THE LONG REST

THE LONG REST

Basil Copper

Books have the
power to extend
the mind and tone
the spirit.

Fay & Will Leeds.

Chivers Press • G.K. Hall & Co.
Bath, Avon, England   Thorndike, Maine USA

This Large Print edition is published by Chivers Press, England, and by G.K. Hall & Co., USA.

Published in 1994 by arrangement with Robert Hale Limited.

U.K. Hardcover ISBN 0–7451–2373–2 (Chivers Large Print)
U.K. Softcover   ISBN 0–7451–2389–9 (Camden Large Print)
U.S. Softcover   ISBN 0–8161–7420–0 (Nightingale Series Edition)

The text of this Large Print edition is unabridged.
Other aspects of the book may vary from the original edition.

Set in 16pt New Times Roman.

Printed in the U.K. on acid-free paper.

British Library Cataloguing in Publication Data available

Library of Congress Cataloging-in-Publication Data

Copper, Basil.
  The long rest / Basil Copper.
     p.   cm.
  ISBN 0–8161–7421–0 (alk. paper : lg. print)
  1. Large type books.   I. Title.
[PR6053.O658L65   1994]   94–12705
823′.914—dc20

CHAPTER ONE

1

'My,' Stella said. 'We are smart today.'

I sat back at my battered old broadtop and stared at the cracks in the ceiling.

'Don't let it fool you,' I said. 'It's just to impress the clients.'

'It impresses me,' Stella said. 'Which is saying something.'

The gold bell of her hair glistened under the overhead lamp as she looked at me with very blue eyes.

I was wearing a new lightweight tweed hacking jacket, cut in London, with fawn slacks and a new pair of tan brogues on my size nines. I'd had quite a good quarter and I'd splashed out on the outfit in a weak moment the previous Saturday night. I felt like Pierre Cardin's top male model at Stella's words. She looked at me mischievously.

'You won't want coffee then? You'll only be spilling it over your trousers.'

I looked at her with narrowed eyes. She looked even better now that I was focusing with more accuracy.

'Don't let all this elegance fool you,' I said. 'There's a lot of squalor around underneath.'

She grinned and went on over to the alcove behind the ground-glass screen where we do the brewing-up. I sat back and listened to the snick of the percolator going on.

There was a steady hum of stalled traffic coming up from the boulevard outside now and the smog and the gasoline fumes were making a nice patina against the dirty glass of the window. It was dark outside despite the fact that it was only mid-morning and it looked like rain again. Some people got tired of the cool rains of winter in L.A. but I liked them. They freshened up the atmosphere and the gurgle of water down the storm-drains during stake-out cases formed some of my most enduring memories.

Your poetic soul is taking over again, Mike, I told myself. Stella came back from the alcove and looked down at me ruminatively. Today she wore a fetching outfit of tartan trews with a heavy leather belt that emphasized her flat stomach and threw into high relief the firmness of her breasts beneath the tan silk shirt with the blue scarf at her brown throat. I wished it didn't. It wasn't the morning for it. Leastways, not in my book. I needed Technicolor to do justice to her.

'You know there's a couple of reports for you to sign, Mike.'

I nodded.

'I know. I'll get to them later.'

Stella sighed and tapped with a gold pencil

against very white teeth.

'The sooner they go out the sooner you get paid,' she said.

'That's different,' I said. 'Let's have them.'

She went over to her own desk and took them out a cardboard file holder. She came and put them down on my blotter. I scribbled my signature above the typed details at the bottom of each sheet. Stella looked at me with faint surprise.

'Aren't you going to read them and check them out?'

I shrugged.

'What for? It would only be a waste of time. They're always immaculate.'

Stella looked at me suspiciously.

'Flattery's off this morning. I'm clean out of biscuits, if that's what you're after.'

I gave her a long look.

'I'm after more than biscuits, honey.'

I sat and admired her flush all the way back to the alcove. She came back and put the full cup on my blotter, pushed over the sugar. She sat down opposite me, in the client's chair and crossed her legs. I went on stirring, uncomfortably aware of the scrutiny of those frank eyes.

'Shouldn't you be getting those reports ready for off?' I said.

She smiled satirically.

'After. This is my coffee break, remember?'

Before I could think anything up the phone

3

buzzed. Stella reached over and picked it off my desk.

'Faraday Investigations. Yes, just a moment.'

She cupped the mouthpiece with her hand and turned to me.

'You know anyone called Ingolstadt?'

'Come again,' I said.

A weary expression passed across Stella's smooth forehead.

'Ingolstadt,' she said.

'I thought it was a town in Germany,' I said.

'He won't say what he wants,' Stella said. 'Except that he needs your help.'

'Didn't you tell him it was my coffee break too?' I said.

Stella grinned. It seemed to light up the whole office.

'You want to keep on eating, don't you? This might be the answer. Then you can buy a new shirt to replace that frayed thing and a tie instead of that gravy-stain pattern card you've got hanging round your neck.'

'Thanks a lot,' I said. 'I make the gags around here.'

She had a point though. I reached over for the phone and took it from her.

A guttural voice sounded in my ear.

'Mr Faraday? I have a little job for you.'

'Not so fast,' I said. 'What sort of little job. I'd like to know something about it first.'

The owner of the voice clicked his teeth with

4

annoyance.

'I am a lawyer, Mr Faraday. I don't fool around. You can look me up in the book if you suspect my bona fides.'

I gave a heavy sigh.

'I don't suspect anything or anyone, Mr Ingolstadt. I'd just like an idea of what your problem is.'

He clicked his teeth again. He could have got a steady job as a castanet manipulator with the resident rumba band over at the Coconut Grove.

'You don't understand, Mr Faraday. This is a highly confidential matter. Believe me, if you can come over to Coniston Avenue it will be to your advantage.'

Stella was already looking up the location on the large-scale. She came back, picked up my empty cup and took it over toward the alcove. Like always, it had been the best cup of the day.

'In what way?' I said.

There was another irritated clicking from the other end of the wire. I was beginning to enjoy this now.

'Money, Mr Faraday. You've heard of it?'

I grinned.

'I remember the stuff, sure.'

'Well then, get on over here,' the voice went on.

Stella was back now, putting the second cup down on my blotter. I looked at it thoughtfully.

'It will pay you,' Ingolstadt put in, like he could read my thoughts.

'Be over in half an hour,' I said.

I put the phone down before he could make with the castanets again.

2

Ingolstadt's office was a rather classy-layout in an off-boulevard location back of Coniston. It was in a private courtyard development and I slotted my five-year-old powder-blue Buick into the only space left at the edge of the parking lot which held about five or six automobiles at most. I killed the motor, frowned at the darkening sky and set fire to a cigarette. I sat and smoked it, listening to a news bulletin on the radio, and watching the drops of rain that were beginning to star the windshield.

I ground out my butt in the end, got my raincoat from the passenger seat beside me and put it over my shoulders. I locked the car and sprinted over toward the entrance steps of Ingolstadt's building. It was bucketing down now and already thin puddles were forming, churned up by the fury of the dancing shards of water. I got in under the canopy of the eight-storey office building and a smart-looking commissionaire wearing one of Marshal Timoshenko's cast-off uniforms, held the door back for me.

'Damp,' he said brightly.

'I hadn't noticed,' I told him, wringing out my trouser-cuffs.

My grin lasted me all the way to the seventh floor.

Werner, Ingolstadt and Marrowby had a nice suite of offices in a style that I thought had gone out with The House Of Seven Gables. There were three big mahogany doors leading on to the corridor, two blank; the other with the legend in gold curlicue script: RECEPTION. I went on in to find deep pile carpeting; oak-panelled walls; some good oil-paintings in gilt frames and discreet mahogany furniture; an oak-railed reception area.

I looked for the quill-pens and Bob Cratchit but he didn't seem to be around today. The rain was streaming down the windows nicely now but green-shaded lamps scattered about made the place look like the more luxurious side of Dickens; and a water cooler, some filing cabinets and several electric typewriters reminded me I was still in the twentieth century.

There were several women in here, mostly early twenties models with figures that went straight all the way down and sensible, mannish suits. The only exception was a tall blonde like Eve Arden in her heyday who was just coming out a door in back. She gave me a thirty-thousand mega-watt smile.

'You're Mr Faraday?'

'I never denied it,' I said.

She gurgled to herself for a moment or two like I'd said something funny. Mrs and Miss Fudd at the far side of Reception looked slightly shocked. It was a bit risqué for this type of atmosphere come to think of it.

'Mr Ingolstadt's anxious to see you, Mr Faraday,' the girl went on when she'd calmed down a little.

'What's he like?' I said.

The blonde number lowered her voice and leaned toward me. I saw her name on a gold-painted plaque on her desk. It was Shelley Beeching. It suited her.

'He's a difficult man,' she said. 'We have trouble keeping him sweet.'

'That so?' I said. 'Any reason why I should?'

The girl shrugged. She wore a fairly short grey skirt and a rust-coloured silk shirt, with a gold chain and ornament hanging round her neck. Apart from Stella she was the nicest thing I'd seen this morning.

'None at all, Mr Faraday,' she said. 'But you might find it pays. He's got a lot of pull around town. And he has a lot of say with the Licensing Commission.'

'You don't say,' I said. 'I'm beginning to tremble already.'

The girl pursed her lips and looked at me with very brown eyes.

'You're not taking me seriously, Mr

8

Faraday,' she said accusingly.

'You don't look a serious girl, Miss Beeching,' I said.

The other two women started typing suddenly. I heard a heavy footfall from one of the far doors. I looked toward them but no-one came out.

'Serious enough,' the girl went on, answering my question.

'Your colleagues seem to take Mr Ingolstadt for real,' I said.

The Beeching job had a slight curl on her lips now.

'Oh, them. They're frightened of their shadows. We use them for typing legal documents. I'm the old man's personal assistant. I trained as a lawyer but decided not to practice.'

'A pity,' I said. 'It would have livened things up downtown.'

'Perhaps,' she said moodily.

We were interrupted by more heavy footsteps. This time they seemed to come from behind one of the other doors. One of the grey-haired women got up and scuttled over, rapped deferentially on the panel and disappeared.

'What's going on?' I said.

'That's Mr Werner's way of summoning a secretary,' the girl said languidly. She was pretending to examine one of her immaculately buffed nails but she wasn't making a very

9

convincing job of it.

'You could have fooled me,' I said. 'I thought they were breaking in a new song and dance act for vaudeville.'

This time the girl did smile.

'I think you'd better go on in, before you entirely disrupt the routine of the office, Mr Faraday. Third on the right.'

I did like she said. She was actually laughing as I got to the door.

CHAPTER TWO

1

Old man Ingolstadt, when I got to see him, looked like he'd been blown out of a jet aircraft backward. He was about sixty-five but looked as solid and strong as a rock. His wind-blown aspect came entirely from his hair and his eyebrows. Both were silver; the hair fell forward in unkempt locks over his eyes so that at all times he looked like he was in need of the services of an expert thatcher. His eyebrows went every which way.

For the rest he had a skin like tanned parchment; deep, humorous eyes which blinked behind gold-rimmed pince-nez attached to a black cord; and whenever his thin

10

lips opened they revealed strong yellow teeth. For the rest he wore a conservative dark suit which was well cut but hung loosely on his big frame and an old-fashioned-looking bow tie evidently cut by Oliver Wendell Holmes' tailor, which was blue with white polka dots.

'Well, well, Mr Faraday,' he rumbled heartily, getting up to shake me enthusiastically by the hand. 'This is an honour, sir.'

I figured he'd been seeing too many old Lionel Barrymore movies but I didn't tell him that.

'We'd better reserve judgment,' I said.

He stared at me for a moment, then burst into a hacking laugh.

'That's good, Mr Faraday. That's good. Reserve judgment! Please sit down.'

He waved me expansively into a chair. I was getting the measure of him already. He was putting on his hammy courtroom manner now. I looked at him warily. Something of my thoughts must have crossed his own mind because he modified his dialogue.

'Highly confidential matter, Mr Faraday. I understand you're a first-class man.'

'That's not for me to say,' I said. 'If you don't like my work, don't pay me.'

He stopped suddenly, like I'd punched him in the ribs and gave me a shrewd look from underneath his shaggy eyebrows.

'That's fair. I like your cut, sir.'

11

'What's your problem,' I said.

He held up a hand, the back of which was thickly covered with white fur.

'Not so fast. We haven't talked terms yet.'

'I never talk terms,' I said. 'I like to hear the situation first.'

He looked at me with genuine shock in his eyes.

'You must be a poor man, Mr Faraday.'

'I am, Mr Ingolstadt,' I said. 'I'm also an honest one.'

There was a glare in his eye now and I held his glance until he looked away. He snorted in the deep silence of the office, which was heavily panelled and got up like the reception suite. Most of the walls were taken up by leather-bound law volumes.

'You're a damned proud one too,' he said.

There was some bitterness in his voice and I looked at him in surprise.

'Is there anything wrong with that?'

He shook his head impatiently.

'Perhaps. Perhaps not. Stiff-necked people cause a lot of trouble.'

I started to get up.

'Then don't employ me, Mr Ingolstadt. It's as simple as that.'

'Sit down, young man!'

The old man's voice cracked like a whip. I grinned. I sat down again. After a moment or two he gave me a roguish grin too.

'By God, I can see we're going to rub against

12

one another. We're two of a kind. But I like your cut, sir.'

'Stop praising yourself,' I said, 'and tell me what you want me to do.'

He stopped in surprise, laid a finger alongside his nose and sniggered.

'It's a simple matter, Mr Faraday. I just want you to deliver a package for me. For that I'm willing to pay you three thousand dollars.'

2

There was a long silence between us. I was smiling now which seemed to make him angry.

'I wish you'd share the joke, sir. You seem to find my proposition absurd. You have a moral objection to money?'

'Not at all,' I told him. 'It's just that I want to know what I'm getting into. You could have got any delivery service to take on your package for a few dollars.'

He shook his head.

'There's a little more to it than that, Mr Faraday.'

'I thought there might be,' I said.

Old man Ingolstadt rummaged around in his desk and came up with a flat parcel that was wrapped in brown paper. It was sealed with sellotape as well as tied round with string and there were big blobs of scarlet wax on the knots of the string. Ingolstadt hefted it in his hand

13

and looked at it solemnly like it contained a gold bar. Then the eyes fixed me from under the white tufts.

'You carry a gun, Mr Faraday?'

'Sometimes,' I said cautiously.

'But you're licensed for it,' he persisted.

'Sure,' I said. 'You think I might need it on this delivery job?'

'Possibly,' he said.

He handed me the package. It was fairly light and I looked at it curiously. Then I turned it over. There was no name or address on either side.

'I'm supposed to guess the recipient?' I said.

The old lawyer turned his eyes up to the ceiling.

'Plenty of humour on this case we got,' he told the light-fitting.

He focused his eyes on me again.

'You heard of Sternwood?'

It was my turn to be surprised.

'The racketeer?'

Ingolstadt's eyes were pained now.

'You must be more tactful when you're in these offices, Mr Faraday. Mr Sternwood is a large-scale businessman and entrepreneur whose activities take in the whole of the L.A. basin.'

'I'll bet,' I said.

There was the pained expression in the eyes again.

'Then you don't want the job? Your high

moral standards again?'

'I didn't say so,' I said. 'I'd just like to know a little more about it. Where have I got to deliver the package, for example.'

'In the L.A. area, of course. If it was out of town I'd have employed someone else.'

'And that's all you're going to tell me?' I said.

The old man spread his hands wide on the blotter.

'That's all you'll need to know,' he said. 'It's the nicest, easiest three thousand dollars you'll ever make.'

'Maybe,' I said. 'If I live to collect it.'

The wary eyes were drilling into mine.

'What makes you say that?'

I shrugged.

'You hinted it was gun-stuff. You must have some reason. Sternwood operates all over the L.A. basin, yes. And bodies have been found all over the L.A. basin too.'

Ingolstadt looked like he was going to blow up but he controlled himself in time.

'Rumours, legends. Every big operator like Sternwood accretes such stories. Fired employees tell disgruntled tales. Contractors frozen off jobs have their axes to grind.'

'Don't try that old stale courtroom stuff on me, Mr Ingolstadt,' I said. 'If I'm doing this job for you I'd like you to level.'

The white thatch was viciously rumpled as he scratched his sixty-five-year-old fingers around in it.

'You're difficult, Mr Faraday.'

'We're both difficult,' I said.

He sighed.

'All right. Perhaps this will quieten your doubts. Sternwood is a big man, like I said. He has lots of enemies, like every big man.'

'Not every big man,' I said. 'St Francis of Assisi. Leonardo da Vinci. Gandhi.'

Ingolstadt crowed with triumph.

'Gandhi was assassinated,' he said quietly.

I didn't argue with him. I'd walked into that one.

'Sternwood is holed out where no-one can reach him,' the old man went on. 'Just as soon as you agree to my proposition I'll contact him. When you've agreed I'll give you his location.'

I nodded, my brows wrinkled with thought. I could have done with a cigarette but I'd heard Ingolstadt was a strict non-smoker and wouldn't allow the habit in his offices.

'What's in the package?' I said.

'Evidence needed to clear him from a murder charge,' Ingolstadt said. 'There's nothing off-colour about this assignment.'

I made up my mind. I reached for the package.

'I'll go home and pick up my gun,' I said.

CHAPTER THREE

1

When I got outside Shelley Beeching was waiting for me with a buff envelope. She put it in my hand.

'The details are in here, Mr Faraday,' she said. 'After you've memorized the address, burn it. Mr Ingolstadt was most insistent on that.'

She looked at me quickly.

'Don't burn the other enclosure. It contains your cheque.'

'I never quite do that,' I said.

I put the envelope in the inner pocket of my jacket.

'What's this all about?' I said.

The girl looked at me shrewdly.

'I thought Mr Ingolstadt just briefed you.'

'We both know better,' I said. 'You're his Girl Tuesday, sure. But you can level with me.'

She shook her head with amusement.

'We both do know better, Mr Faraday. You better than to ask me. Me better than to tell you. I'll see you when you come back.'

'If I come back,' I said. 'This gets more like Boys' Espionage Stories every minute.'

She held out a brown hand for me to shake.

'Only if you make it so, Mr Faraday. Don't forget to burn that stuff.'

I looked at her steadily.

'You know, Miss Beeching,' I said. 'Old man Ingolstadt forgot to click his teeth even once all the time I was in there. He must have been really nervous about this assignment.'

I went out carrying the small package, leaving her standing there in a silence as deep as the Mariana Trench.

I'd picked up my raincoat from the outer office and I slipped it on again in the vestibule as it was still sheeting down outside. I got over to the Buick in a flat sprint and dropped behind the wheel with water running nicely down my hair and into my collar. I put the package on the passenger seat by my side, making sure the other door was locked. It lay there innocuously. By its size and shape it looked as though it might be a small notebook or ledger.

It was no business of mine, anyway. Leastways, it was really, but old man Ingolstadt hadn't chosen to make it so. He'd conned me nicely into taking on what might turn out to be a very dubious assignment. I lit a cigarette and sat smoking for a while, gnawing over the problem. That didn't help any so I tore open the buff envelope the Beeching number had given me.

Like she said it contained two enclosures; both smaller buff envelopes, both sealed with sellotape. One of them had my name typed on

18

it. When I opened it I found a mauve cheque-form inside, made out to me for the prescribed amount and signed in old man Ingolstadt's spidery writing, against his printed name. I noticed that the cheque had also been counter-signed by Shelley Beeching against another printed line which also gave her title as company secretary.

I raised my eyebrows, frowning at the rain starring the windscreen. Quite a high-powered lady, Mike, I told myself. I put the cheque back in the envelope and the whole thing in my inner jacket pocket. I let the second envelope lie a minute or two while I finished off my cigarette. I opened it to a distinct feeling of anti-climax. I don't know what I expected but there was nothing in there except a single sheet of high-class notepaper, without even a letter-heading.

Typed in the middle of the sheet of paper, without any mention of the man's name, a signature or any superscription, was merely an address; not more than half a dozen words in all.

I slid the metal ash-tray from the dash and moodily stubbed out my cigarette-butt. The interior of the Buick was filled with the distinctive smell of stale air, damp leather and old cigarette-smoke. I cautiously lowered the driving window half an inch and got some fresh stuff circulating.

The address was off Durango Drive, way up in the hills on the edge of town. I got out my large-scale from the dashboard cubby and memorized the route. It would take me a little while to get up there from my present location. I decided to take an early lunch and ring Stella to let her know the score. Not Ingolstadt's confidential stuff, of course, but just my destination. In case anything happened. I checked my watch. It was a nuisance but Ingolstadt had given me a pretty broad hint.

I decided instead to make for my rented house over on Park West, break the Smith-Wesson .38 out of the small armoury I keep in a locked bedroom cupboard over there. I sighed. That meant frying myself up something for lunch at home. It was a system never too popular with me. I'm no Cesar Ritz. I looked at the address again. I figured I could remember it all right.

I put the envelope and the single sheet in the metal dashboard tray. I lit a match and set fire to the edges of the sheets. When they were nicely incinerated, I raked around in the tray with the match-stalk until they were nothing but dark powder. Then I shut the tray, sneered at the rain, started the motor and eased on out. I started making time toward Park West.

2

I was on my way out soon after three p.m. The weather was no better but at least I had

20

something inside me; I was reasonably dry; I was on my second after-lunch cigarette and I had the radio while I drove. Just marginally it was one of the better days. I found the crossing I wanted, waited until the lights changed, and tooled up into the right section, the Smith-Wesson making a nice pressure against my chest muscles in its nylon webbing harness as I spun the wheel.

I wondered what Ingolstadt's game was. He hadn't told me anything really. Not half of anything. The whole thing smelt. If Sternwood was behind this and the old man was working for him I was likely to get my ass shot off for my trouble. And what was in the package that was so important; so important it couldn't be posted or delivered by the usual channels? He was paying me well, of course; there was no denying that.

And I could certainly do with the money. But people like Ingolstadt don't give that sort of money away for such easy assignments. There was a big trick here somewhere and I was missing it for the moment.

Even Stella had jibbed a little when I'd told her the bare facts; she was a girl with her head screwed on the right way. I'd put her off with a bromide but she'd want to know more when I got back to the office. I wondered whether to tell her everything the old man had told me.

I guessed maybe I would tell her and get her reaction. After all, Ingolstadt hadn't actually made me promise not to tell anyone within my own organization; such as it was.

He'd merely asked me to keep it confidential. You're prevaricating again, Mike, I told myself. My, we're making with the big words today. I was so busy grinning I almost missed my next turning and had to brake rather harder than I'd intended. Conditions were nasty and there was a lot of slurry on the road from contracting operations up ahead.

The sky was as dark as a mortician's hatband and there was plenty more rain up there. The wind was gusting the higher I went and I could hear the heavy shudder of water on the chassis of the car clear above the soft braying of saxophones coming from the radio. I'd asked Stella to do a check on Sternwood and find out his latest activities; his public ones, at any rate, and I'd no doubt she'd have something ready for me by the time I got back in.

That was about all I could do for the moment. I guessed maybe Sternwood's political or racketeering opponents—it was rather a twilight area here and they tended to merge into one another—were gunning for him and I didn't aim to get in the middle. But that was undoubtedly the score. Which was the reason for Ingolstadt mentioning artillery and for the high tab on the job.

I was on the secondary road I wanted and the tyres were drumming monotonously on the metalled surface and throwing up sheets of water which was lying around in large puddles. I had my side-lights on but now I switched to main-beam because the road was twisting up the side of the canyon and forest-land was coming down close, making a dark tunnel through which the Buick was boring. It was getting on for dusk anyway.

If anything the rain was heavier than when I started; it certainly can rain in California and today was about the worst day I could have chosen for such an assignment. Then I remembered the cheque burning a hole in my breastpocket, which considerably tempered the hardships.

There were heavy belts of fir, sycamore and spruce here and it was almost as dark as night because I couldn't see the sky through the interlacing branches. I stopped for a moment and looked at my large-scale by the dash-lights. I saw I was still on the right track and went on more slowly, making for a clearing in the forest where there was a stone obelisk and a finger-post which should give me my direction.

There wasn't much traffic on the road either way this time of the afternoon but I'd been conscious the last few minutes of lights in rear of me. They might be quite innocuous but they gnawed at me and when they turned off at the next fork and kept pace with me about a hundred yards behind, faint alarm bells began ringing way down in my subconscious.

It was a lonely section out here and I'd made my living and kept on living either by keeping out of trouble; or being prepared for it when it came. Today was no exception. I figured I had a mile to go for the cross-roads and that would be the clincher. I glanced in the mirror a few times but the other vehicle was keeping the same distance, and it was too dark and the rear window too misted by rain to make out any details.

The yellow beams of my headlights were scything through the darkness and now they picked out the bleached whiteness of the cross-roads; there was the big cairn I remembered. The white finger-post sat atop of it and I slowed, winding down the passenger window to make out the direction I wanted. The other car, a big saloon passed me then, going pretty fast and turned off round the obelisk, disappearing from sight.

I made out the reference for Durango and turned off right, the Buick shuddering over the rutted forest road. I had just got straightened up when I saw the main-beams of the other car turn up after me too. There was no doubt it was the same vehicle. There had been no sign of anything else up here for the past few minutes and the driver had undoubtedly turned right round the obelisk, parked without lights and then followed on when he saw which direction I was taking.

I got out the Smith-Wesson from the

24

shoulder holster and laid it down on the passenger-seat at my side, after throwing off the safety. I had a spare clip, making ten shots in all. I slightly relaxed my lips. Another car had circled the obelisk and followed me; maybe he had merely lost his way and had now picked up his route again. Maybe. But it was still no reason for behaving like World War Three had broken out.

You're getting jittery, Mike, I told myself. You're thirty-three years old and getting soft too. We would see. I pulled the Smith-Wesson a little closer to hand and concentrated on the steering.

The road was narrowing now as it went farther uphill and the trees came down in a tangled mass, making it darker than ever. It was a bad place to be trapped but there was nowhere else to turn around and nowhere else to go but onward unless I wanted to risk stopping.

I decided against that. I was coming to a metal bridge now, which spanned a stream which was coming down white and fierce as it was torn to fragments by the rocks. I guessed it was swollen by the heavy rains recently and possibly fed by one of the lakes up in the hills. The road went straight away from the bridge and started to turn and go steeply uphill.

I drew the Buick to a crawl and looked in the rear mirror. The car behind had stopped now and its main beams went off, the sidelights looking like two eyes in the gloom. There was another finger-post by the side of the road which pointed upward; it had painted on it in black letters the name of the property I wanted. I squinted at it. It looked pretty temporary to me; just a piece of rough wood shoved into the ground, with a shingle tacked to it with the crudely lettered words. The last of the words was even running with the rain which proved it had only been painted very recently. I smelt a very big rat then. It was getting dark now and this was a bad place to be.

There was a heavy stand of timber at the roadside here, which not only provided shelter from the rain but would also give shelter of another sort with the heavy trunks of the trees. What was even better was that there was a track through the trees which led to a small clearing where I might turn round in emergency. I felt I had to get off the road fast.

I looked back. The sidelights of the other car were still there. The roaring of the stream was in my ears as I got the Buick quickly off the hard surface and jolted down the track. I felt better once I'd got the screen of trees between us and I turned, facing the way I'd come. I drove quickly back and re-parked in the shadows.

I got out the car, clutching the small package and put it in my raincoat pocket. I got back on the road, feeling very vulnerable as I walked on down past the finger-post. There was a dark

26

sedan slewed across the road as I got to the bend. It was just the other side and the occupants must have been taken by surprise for they were just getting out when I showed. I looked for the house but I couldn't see one.

'Who's there?' the first man called.

'Faraday,' I said. 'I'm expected.'

'Sure, Faraday,' the second one gritted. 'You're expected.'

There was an odd silence. I was standing about halfway between the bridge and the parked sedan now, with the first vehicle a long way back. The Buick was a lot nearer to me, of course; about ten yards off, among the trees. I stepped slowly back toward it, holding the Smith-Wesson in my right-hand raincoat pocket.

The mainbeam of the parked car back along the track suddenly hit me, stencilling my silhouette across the road ahead. That was when the shooting started.

CHAPTER FOUR

1

I felt lead whistle by so close it seemed to scorch my cheek. Fear gave me hair-trigger reactions. I went over backward in the dirt at the side of the road. I had the Smith-Wesson clear and snapped a shot off as I landed, heard it strike the body of the slewed sedan with a loud tearing of metal. The two men scattered, cursing.

I had turned now and was slithering back along the edge of the track in the shadow of the trees, the roaring of the stream beginning to mask the crack of shots. A bullet struck a tree-trunk a dozen feet away from me but it was obviously only random firing. I had to make my shots tell. I was up near the Buick now, soaked, with my heart pumping spasmodically but my reflexes working nicely.

I hoped the two parties would keep on firing. Maybe they'd cancel out if they kept on. Possibly the same thought occurred to them because the shooting stopped abruptly. The yellow headlamp beams shining down the road handicapped me and made me feel vulnerable. I got off another shot, aiming very carefully at the left-hand headlight.

There was a tinkle of glass and the right went out. There were muffled shouts and then the other was extinguished. I grunted to myself. No prizes for accuracy this afternoon, Faraday. But then the conditions were atrocious for this sort of thing. I got away from the Buick and down into a small draw which led underneath the bridge.

From there I was concealed myself but could see if the two parties decided to join forces on the road. I had a distinct advantage all the time I was off the road because they couldn't see me and the only danger I ran in here would be from an accidental ricochet. There was a lull for a couple of minutes and while that was going on, I got behind the bushes and re-loaded.

That still left me with eight and I figured I'd already made more use of mine than they had. I had some pretty bleak thoughts as I crouched in the mud with the rain coursing down my neck. I wondered if old man Ingolstadt could hear me. His ears would have dropped off.

I heard a bough break underfoot somewhere then and froze. I could hear the sound of a car being driven slowly and the sidelights of the automobile that had followed me crawled up toward the bridge. It stopped a couple of yards away and someone got down because I could see a shadow pass across the sidelights. Then the motor cut out again. There was nothing happening now except the pattering of the rain on hundreds of acres of soaking foliage. A great day, Mike, I told myself.

It was quite dark now and I had to do something soon because it wouldn't take more than a few moments for these characters to immobilize the Buick. Once they did that I'd be finished. They could then hunt me through the woods at leisure. Of course, I could simply disappear and leave my heap. But conversely, I could wander for days in this deserted section

29

of mountains. And if I didn't die of pneumonia eventually I might easily break a leg and starve to death.

The prospects weren't good and the more I thought about it the more I felt my resolution oozing away. It's difficult to reason properly and make firm decisions when you're cold and water is dripping steadily through your clothing and soaking your body. I heard another branch crackle. I moved, keeping in thick cover. Unless I was as heavy-footed as the character who was clumping around out there, no-one would hear me, as small noises were masked by the heavy rain.

I decided to keep working up toward the bridge. On the road there was room for two vehicles to pass; but the bridge narrowed and if they thought to park on it they would completely block my escape route. I could go on uphill, of course, but for all I knew the road might peter out in a clearing. Somehow, I figured the estate mentioned by Ingolstadt didn't exist. The temporary notice-board pointed toward it. The more I thought about the set-up, the screwier it seemed.

I was working up the draw now; there were heavy boulders in here and sheets of water coming down the hillsides were making a miniature stream which was about two feet deep and following the bed of the ravine, so I had to be careful. I put the Smith-Wesson away, after wiping it carefully with my handkerchief. There was no sense in risking getting it too wet. I didn't want a misfire, whatever happened. I wouldn't get a second chance.

I could hear voices now. The bridge was in sight. There was no-one on it but I could see the dim shapes of two men standing at the edge of the road a few yards from the bridge entrance. The big car was just beyond them. The stream itself was roaring in my ears as it tumbled over boulders about ten yards ahead of me. I couldn't get across it, had no intention of trying. But if I could work up toward the edge of the bank, at the nearest point to the bridge itself there might be a chance of something.

The voices were louder. The men must have been half-shouting over the sound of the stream. There were three now, all big, and all dressed in anonymous dark-coloured slickers. They seemed undecided what to do. Fortunately there were boulders at the edge of the stream here and I worked my way up behind them, conscious of the water pouring down my collar and into my shoes. I'd never felt so dirty and uncomfortable in my life. Which was saying a great deal. So much for my new outfit.

I'd got as far as I could go. I was in darkness down here but there was a little light up on the road. I was deafened by the thunder of the stream and it boiled past green and white as it was gashed by the boulders only some five or

31

six feet in front of me. It was bringing down small tree branches and other debris and it smelt cold and cruel in the semi-gloom. I got out the Smith-Wesson again and balanced it against the sloping edge of the rock in front of me.

The three men had slightly shifted back toward the big car, as though its bulk comforted them. They were still arguing about something but naturally I couldn't make out the words. I felt the package then, awkward and constraining in my raincoat pocket. I moved into a more comfortable position, concentrating on my aim. The vehicle was quite near the edge of the lane and I could just about clear the road-edge to reach the chassis. The range was all right too. I'd try three shots initially, to see what happened, ignoring the men. I wouldn't get a second chance and I had to make it good.

I squeezed the trigger, got off a pattern of three, shifting slightly over each time. The muzzle-flame seemed to spread out from the barrel of the Smith-Wesson and then back toward me in an eye-aching dazzle of incandescence.

2

The explosion reached me a few seconds later, seemed to knock me flat with the concussion. I

32

rolled over, the stream and the brush around me as light as day. The tank had gone up and the heat was so terrific, even here on the other side of the stream, that some branches of the overhanging trees on this bank had caught fire. The screams were swiftly choked out, like someone snuffing a candle.

A blazing torch jumped over the bridge railing, was extinguished in the dark water, as it tumbled among the boulders. A bundle of charred clothing within a pillar of white fire collapsed on the roadway, like the wick of a lamp. I couldn't see the third man, didn't want to see. The automobile went on blazing, the flames forty feet in the air now, like they would go on for ever. There must have been a full tank.

I was back in behind the bushes, my nostrils choked by the sickly aroma of grilled flesh. I swiftly re-loaded, aware of a heavy body blundering about on my side of the stream. The noise went back up toward the road. I could hear faint cries now and the pounding of heavy boots on tarmac. It was time to move. There would never be a better.

I went through the bushes and over the rocks in a rush, hardly caring what noise I made. No-one had any time left for me at the moment. I orientated myself by the reflected light up on the road and quickly worked my way along toward where I'd left the Buick. I was more cautious now, though my heart was

33

still pounding. I held the Smith-Wesson down within my raincoat pocket, to keep the wet out, safety-catch off. I'd fire through the pocket if anyone came at me. This was no time for sartorial elegance.

I worked up the hillside, slithering among the scree and the boulders, wishing I'd taken up some other occupation. I was near the Buick now, in the gloom of the trees, though shouts were still coming from the road and the glare of the fire was reflecting along the shrubbery at the verge. It must have generated terrific heat now and I knew it would go on until there were only a few pieces of tangled metal and panelwork left.

I kept my eyes peeled, stabbing glances left and right through the gloom. A heavy boot gritted on the road surface and I froze. There was a big man standing near the Buick, evidently on guard in case I returned. He was on the road, looking down toward the fire, with his back toward me. A big man, with a thick neck and shoulders as broad as a bull. I got the other side of the Buick, my movements masked by the steady drumming of the rain. I went along at ground level.

The car tyres were intact at any rate. I guessed they hadn't had time to do anything, other than keep my heap under surveillance. When I was sure there was only the one man around, I worked in back again. The man on guard was still completely engrossed in the action down by the burning car. It was only about a minute and a half since the explosion but it seemed a hell of a long time to me.

I eased up the other side of the Buick. The tyres were all right here as well. I had to have that information if I was going to do anything. I circled and went around once more. I quietly tried the driving door. It was still unlocked as I'd left it. That was another thing it was vital to know. While I was doing that I saw the big man turn around and face in my direction. I ducked, hoping he hadn't seen anything.

I heard boots grate on the gravel again then, kept low. A faint shadow came between me and the glare of the fire. I looked beneath the chassis of the Buick, keeping down to the ground. The big man was standing motionless, facing me. He was evidently uneasy about something. Perhaps he had heard the faint click as I'd opened the door. The footsteps sounded again. He was coming over. I melted back toward the rear of the car. He crossed over in front of the bonnet, walking slowly, peering about him. I guessed then he wasn't used to the country. He seemed to start at every slight noise made by the rain dripping off leaves.

I crouched down by the boot and held my breath. The man in the dark belted raincoat came hesitantly round the bonnet of the Buick. He paused by the driving door, looked carefully around him again, turning his head nervously from side to side. Then he bent and tried the door, shoved his head inside. I thought for a moment he was going to sit in which would have made things difficult, to say the least. Then there was another shout from down the road.

He straightened up and slammed the door. He looked nervously around him once again. If he came toward the rear of the car I would have to double quickly along the other side and hope he wouldn't spot me. But then I would be against the light. It could be difficult. His boots made a squelching noise in the mud. His shadow moved away.

I risked a quick glance. He was going around the bonnet again, back the way he'd come. I quickly got in rear of the Buick and moved up toward the driving door. The big man was at the side of the road, still staring back down the hill. The fire must have still been fierce because I could see the flicker reflected off the wet macadam surface.

There wouldn't be much more time. I got across the intervening space without making much noise; the rain was quite fierce here, out from the shelter of the trees. Even so he must have heard me because he half-turned as I came at him. I chopped him as hard as I knew how with the barrel of the Smith-Wesson. I was aiming behind the ear but I got him in the neck muscle and he grunted with pain. He was already stumbling when I caught him in the right place and he dropped without a sound. I dragged him in the bushes, sweating with the exertion. He must have weighed all of sixteen stone, most of it muscle. I hadn't got time to search him. It wasn't the night for that sort of thing. Nothing else moved in the gloom except for the flickering reflections on the road and the millions of globules of falling water. I got back to the Buick in three seconds flat, closed the door behind me. I kept all the lights off and put my key in the ignition. She started first pull and I roared off the soft earth, the tyres tearing until they found solid road.

I changed gear and went rocketing down the lane, to where gesticulating figures were silhouetted against the flames of the burning auto, going like hell for the narrow bridge.

CHAPTER FIVE

1

I guess they hadn't heard anything at first. They'd gotten branches and were pushing the bodies clear of the wreck. Under normal circumstances I'd have felt some compunction but they'd been out to kill me. It was kill or be killed in such circumstances. I'd wound the driving window down and had the Smith-

Wesson handy but there'd be little chance to use it. I was relying on speed, not fire-power now. I must have been doing almost sixty when I hit the bridge.

It would have been suicidal without lights except that the glare from the fire was etching the lattice-work of the girders in brilliant black and white. I was halfway across when I saw the man. He had a big branch in his hand and he was balancing it to throw. It hit the bonnet of the Buick with a tremendous clatter and there was a shudder as it hit the windshield upright and bounced off. I jinked the steering wheel but there was no room to manoeuvre in such a narrow space.

He gave a thin scream as I hit him and I saw his body bounce like a rag-doll. He was flung over the rail and disappeared into the roaring waters of the stream. Sweat ran down my face and my hands were trembling on the wheel. This was more like World War Three; Ingolstadt hadn't exaggerated. Gun-stuff and then some.

The men round the auto hesitated and then broke as I came at them; they would had to have been superhuman not to have done. I was coming from darkness into light; I wasn't carrying any illumination myself and they were blinded by the flames and no doubt shaky from seeing three men incinerated. I didn't blame them. But I had myself to think of. They had nothing to fire at and I wanted it to stay like that as long as possible.

I jinked the wheel again as I got on to the broader area of road. A dim shadow loomed up. They could see me now and a red flame lanced from the darkness. The side window starred and I got down. Then I was past, my toe on the accelerator until it reached the floorboards.

The glare in the sky behind me receded in the rear-mirror, before it was cut off by the turn of the road. There were two more shots before that but they both went wide.

I got about ten miles down the bluff before I slackened speed. I drew in to the side of the road, wound down the window and got some air. I began to tremble violently and felt sick. I was afraid of vomiting on my cushions so I got out for a couple of minutes. I lit a cigarette and smoked for a while. Strangely enough I didn't notice the rain then. But I began to feel better.

I got back in again and sat until the shaking had stopped. My shoes and trousers were like sodden paper and I was covered with mud. I put my sidelights on and considered the position. Such as it was. Then I remembered the package. I got it out of my raincoat pocket. It was sodden by now. Some of the brown paper had started to peel.

I put it down on the passenger-seat next me and stared at it for long moments. Then I started to undo it. There were several layers of brown paper and then a lot of old newspapers sellotaped together. What I drew out in the end was the article that had given the package its flat, distinctive shape. It was simply a block of ordinary wood, sawn out in a rectangle and absolutely worthless.

It wasn't the first time I'd been made a dummy but it was one of the neatest. For that piece of sawn deal four men had died and I'd nearly been chopped myself. I sat and finished my cigarette and stared at the thing. I was smiling by the time I'd stubbed out my butt in the dashboard ashtray. I gathered up the pieces of the parcel and put them in the dash-cubby. Then I started making time back in to L.A. There were a few questions I wanted answered.

2

I found a pay-phone in a drug-store and got hold of Stella. I gave her an edited version of the proceedings. There was a long, heavy silence on the wire.

'What's Ingolstadt playing at, Mike?' she said in the end.

'There's a nasty echo on the line,' I said. 'Anything on Sternwood and his recent activities?'

'Nothing special,' Stella said. 'You want my report tonight?'

I grinned.

'Tomorrow will do.'

'I'll remember,' Stella said. 'You know Sternwood's currently under investigation?'

'I heard something about it,' I said.

'There's more to it than that,' Stella said. 'His ex-girlfriend is involved. There was some sort of garbled story in the papers a few weeks ago.'

'Thanks, honey,' I said. 'See what else you can dig up.'

'Will do,' she said.

There was a brief silence.

'Take care,' Stella said.

I grinned again.

'Now she tells me.'

I looked at myself in the mirror of the booth. My new clothes were smeared with mud and my eyes looked bleakly out of a dead white face.

'You still there?' Stella said.

'Just about,' I told her.

'I should go home and get some rest,' she said.

I looked at my watch. It had just turned eight o'clock.

'I have too many things to do. You got Ingolstadt's private address?'

'He's got a place over on Carn Brea Drive,' Stella said. 'Hold on.'

She went away and came back. I could hear her riffling pages. She gave me the name and number of the property. I thanked her and rang off. I looked at myself in the mirror again.

41

I felt about a hundred years old. And rheumatic into the bargain.

I got out the booth and back into the Buick. I sat in the driving seat and smoked for a while. The rain was still drumming monotonously down but I was beginning to feel better. The Smith-Wesson made a comforting pressure against my shoulder muscles as I drove on over to Ingolstadt's.

I flipped the radio on and caught a news bulletin. There was no mention of the shoot-out or the casualty figures. Not that I'd have expected there to be. Probably only a forest ranger would be likely to come on the burnt-out wreck. Unless the survivors had tipped it off the road into the stream and buried the bodies somewhere in the forest. That was a distinct possibility.

I worried at the information Stella had given me. I'd been frozen the last hour but now the brain-muscles were beginning to function again. If Sternwood was in trouble I'd be a double dummy to go on sticking my neck out. I'd been a dummy for a long time, of course. Apart from being a punch-bag for hoods and a moving target in the past. But the boys I was up against played for keeps.

They shot first and asked questions later. They'd certainly wanted my package badly. I'd been tailed, of course; but how had the other car-load of trigger-men known my destination? Unless there had been a leak. I remembered Shelley Beeching's highly enigmatic attitude. There had been leaks in lawyers' offices before.

I shook up what was left of my brain and let it sift down with the other debris. I had been so busy beating up the grey matter that I almost missed the turn-off. I was on Carn Brea Drive now and I tooled along, the rain beating heavily on the roof, looking for the number I wanted. It was a modest place by L.A. standards set only in about three acres of landscaped garden and woodland.

I drifted the Buick up the red gravel drive under the light from the ornamental brass lanterns set atop metal poles and crunched to a halt in front of the steps to the porch of the old boy's Gothic mansion. There were lights on in all the windows. I went up the steps quickly, a hard anger beginning to burn inside me, the rain cold and refreshing on my hot face.

I got in under the shadows of the colonnaded porch where another brass lantern burned and rang the bell set in a door so full of stained-glass that it wouldn't have disgraced Notre Dame. The one in Paris, of course. I waited a few seconds, the rain battering at the steps and on the leaded porch roof thinking of wealthy lawyers who employ other people to do the hard graft and wondering why I'd ever gotten into such a life.

I was about to hit the bell again when there was a shuffling at the door and it opened about

43

two inches. A little old lady was standing there, dressed in a starched white maid's apron and a starched cap to match. She looked at me with eyes as bright as a Walt Disney mouse.

'Yes?'

I tried to look debonair but it was difficult in my dishevelled condition.

'Mike Faraday to see Mr Ingolstadt.'

The face expressed disquiet.

'Have you an appointment?'

'Do I look as if I have?' I said. 'Just tell him it's urgent. He'll see me all right.'

The old lady clicked her tongue. I could see where Ingolstadt had got the habit now.

'That's all very well, Mr Faraday, but he has a young lady to dinner.'

'Lucky for him,' I said. 'It's all right to let me in. I'll sign a guarantee against any losses on the family silver if that'll satisfy you.'

There was a strange sound in the porch. The old lady was sniggering. She wiped her eyes with a veined hand, then recollected herself and stared at me severely.

'There's no need for levity, young man. I guess it'll be all right for you to come in.'

I nodded.

'I'm working on a case for Mr Ingolstadt,' I said.

She nodded again and tottered round me, closing the massive mahogany door with a thunderous boom. I was in a vast, marble-floored hall which boasted a spiral staircase, a lot of expensive oil-paintings in gold frames and a few pieces of what looked like genuine Second Empire French furniture.

'He's doing all right for himself,' I said.

The old lady pursed her lips and led me over to a banquette near the foot of the stairs.

'You could say that, Mr Faraday. I'll just announce you if you'll wait a moment.'

'Sure,' I said.

I stood and watched her totter toward big double doors at the far end of the entrance vestibule. I figured she might keel over before she got there but she made it all right. The doors shut softly behind her.

I got out my pack, found a cigarette that wasn't too badly crushed and lit up. I'd been so far out of normal before I hadn't noticed that I must have fallen on them during the shoot-out earlier in the evening. I straightened the tip and drew the smoke gratefully in. It was very quiet in here; so quiet in fact that I could still hear the rain tapping at the windows.

There was a very nice hunting scene in a long frame a little down from where I was standing. I'm no art expert but I figured it for a mid-nineteenth-century English study by one of the minor masters. There were a lot of red-coated hooligans chasing a pack of hounds over hedges and fences; what the hounds were chasing wasn't shown.

Two of the riders had pitched off, one into a very muddy pond; another was being carted away on a hurdle by a group of hunt servants. Seemed like a great way to spend a winter's day. I went over and admired the brushwork. That was about the only admirable thing about it. A gilt plaque underneath said, in black curlicue lettering: A Good Day's Sport. I frowned at it. I should have hated to have been around on one of the bad days.

There was a small silver plate attached a little further along the frame which said, in exquisitely engraved letters: To Lionel Ingolstadt, in appreciation of his very great services extending over forty years. From his friends of the Los Angeles Bar Association.

I turned as the door behind me opened. Strong yellow light from the drawing-room spilled out into the hall.

Ingolstadt stood there, his hands held out melodramatically. He beamed at me, taking in my decrepit condition.

'Excellent, Mr Faraday! The dry run was a great success. You've come through with flying colours!'

CHAPTER SIX

1

'You can save all that guff for your friends of

the Bar Association,' I said. 'Dry run hell! You could wring me out and then still have enough water left over to work the Boulder Dam turbines for another couple of hours.'

The old man's smile broadened.

'My dear Mr Faraday. What do you mean?'

'You know what I mean well enough,' I told him. 'You set me up. You nearly got my butt shot off tonight. And you knew what I was going into.'

Ingolstadt stepped back a little and regarded me frostily.

'That is a little unfair, Mr Faraday,' he protested. 'But we can talk better over a drink. Will you not join us for dinner?'

'That's a little more like it,' I said. 'Unless you feel I'll be lowering the tone of your table.'

I was in the brighter light now and the lawyer's jaw dropped open.

'Good heavens, Mr Faraday. I see what you mean.'

'Do you?' I said. 'There were half a dozen guys out there gunning for me. If I'd have known that I'd have given them that piece of firewood you so thoughtfully wrapped up for me.'

The old man's eyes were twinkling now. He looked at me shrewdly.

'I like you more and more, Mr Faraday. You were the perfect choice.'

'I'm afraid I can't say it's reciprocated,' I said. 'We'll save the explanations for later. I'd

47

like to wash up first.'

'The bathroom is on the second floor,' he began.

'The kitchen will do,' I said. 'If you've no objection. I only want to wash my hands. I'd need a laundry to do justice to the rest.'

Ingolstadt shrugged.

'Just as you wish. But you'd better have that drink first and meet my guest.'

I gave him a long look.

'I didn't want to disturb you but there's some things we've got to talk about. Things that won't wait until morning.'

He put his hand on my shoulder and drew me toward the big drawing-room doors.

'By all means. But come along in. You know the young lady already.'

I blinked in the brighter light in here. It came from a series of crystal chandeliers that marched down the ceiling of the big room that must have been all of sixty feet long. The little old lady was tottering back down the carpeting now, looking as fragile as some of the furniture.

'Mr Faraday would like a full bottle of bourbon, some ice and water, Elvira,' Ingolstadt said in a soothing voice.

'He'll have to get it himself, then,' she snapped. 'I'm about wore out with all the comings and goings at your beck and call.'

Ingolstadt beamed happily.

'She's as strong as a horse,' he told me

calmly.

He turned his head to look after her.

'Let's have no nonsense, Elvira.'

She went away grumbling and he drew me over toward a big marble fireplace where a sweet-scented fire of logs was burning. I sat down on a leather seat at one side of the fireplace and looked at him with narrowed eyes.

'We'll go in in just a minute or two,' he said. 'As soon as my other guest has joined us. I'm sure we can postpone discussion of our business until then.'

'I thought our business was confidential,' I said.

He shook his head.

'It is, Mr Faraday. But I trust the people with whom I am associated as I would myself.'

I looked at him sharply.

'That means you trust me?'

He nodded approvingly.

'Naturally, Mr Faraday. You were specially selected.'

'That's why you set me up and sent me out to be a clay-pigeon,' I said.

He held up his hand soothingly.

'Moderation, Mr Faraday. Moderation in all things. I did warn you to carry a gun. And you have justified my every expectation.'

'I'm glad I pleased somebody,' I said. 'I've had a hell of an evening myself.'

The ancient maid was wheeling a trolley

49

back across the drawing-room now, looking like she was hanging on to the handles to save herself from collapsing. I was halfway across the space toward her when Ingolstadt stopped me with a hand on my arm.

'She's a great actress, Mr Faraday,' he beamed. 'Leave her alone and she'll soon stop her nonsense.'

I went over to avoid any argument and poured myself a liberal shot in the crystal glass, added a little water and plenty of ice.

Ingolstadt himself carried the bottle over toward a table near the fire. He mixed himself a drink, handling the ice-cubes with little silver tweezers shaped like animal's claws. I guessed they were a gift from one of his former clients before he went up to the death-house. But maybe I was being a little hard on him.

The old boy came over to me and chinked the rim of his glass against mine.

'Cheers,' he said, in the English fashion.

'Cheers,' I said.

I wasn't really in a toasting mood but it was difficult to keep up my anger when he was being so hospitable. He probably figured on that. We were standing there, the liquor beginning to trace fingers of fire down into my stomach and my extremities when the drawing-room door opened and a tall, elegantly dressed girl came in.

She looked at me wide-eyed, stayed in the doorway for a moment, and then came down the room toward us, with long, lithe steps.

'Hullo again, Mr Faraday. What disaster area did you spring from?' Shelley Beeching said.

2

Old man Ingolstadt sniggered to himself and I heard a furtive titter from the direction of the drinks trolley. The old lady, Elvira, seemed more like a malevolent gnome than ever.

'I always go swimming with my clothes on,' I said. 'It's more interesting like that.'

The Beeching number smiled gravely, her blonde hair shimmering in the light of the chandeliers, but her eyes were quite serious.

'I'll have my usual, Elvira,' she said. 'You'd better make it a double this evening.'

She looked anxiously at my mud-stained clothing. Ingolstadt intercepted the look.

'The damage to your clothing comes out of your expense account, Mr Faraday,' he said ingratiatingly. 'That is in addition to your fee, of course.'

'It's comforting to know,' I said. 'I take it the same applies to funeral expenses.'

The girl bit her lip but old man Ingolstadt just went on beaming.

'I hardly think it will come to that,' he said complacently.

'We'll see,' I said. 'And now, if you'll excuse

51

me for a minute or two I'll just go wash up.'

'Elvira will show you where,' he said.

The old lady grumbled again but she led the way at a fast enough pace, so I guess her employer knew what he was talking about. She led me to a small cloakroom approached through a door at the bottom of the stairs. If the taps of the wash-basins weren't made of pure gold they were close enough to it. I washed-up and felt better then. I found some toilet paper and cleaned my shoes; sponged off my clothing; straightened my tie; and then washed my hands again. By the time I'd finished I felt I might live another couple of years or so with a little care and kindness.

There was no sign of the old woman as I wandered back through the drawing-room which was now empty. I picked up my drink, replenished the glass and went on over to where voices sounded. There was another pair of sliding-doors on the other side of the room. Beyond them I found a large, shadowy dining-room where Shelley Beeching and her employer sat at a circular table.

There was another big fire in a brick fireplace burning on the other side of the room and the place was full of New England furniture; brass barometers and nautical instruments on tables and hanging on the walls; and here and there eighteenth-century prints of Cape Cod schooners and fishing smacks. Another place had been set for me opposite the others and I sat down to find a good white wine had already been uncorked. Before I could move Elvira was at my elbow, expertly pouring.

The wine was nicely chilled and tasted great. I put down my bourbon near my soup-plate and decided to alternate. Ingolstadt beamed across at me as though my visit was the most everyday thing in the world.

'You see what I meant, Mr Faraday. Miss Beeching is my right hand. In the evenings sometimes she is my lifeline also. Keeping company with an old man; playing chess; joining me for dinner; and advising me as to the right course to take in my cases.'

The girl flushed and looked at me imploringly.

'You really mustn't exaggerate, Mr Ingolstadt.'

He put his hand on hers as it lay on the table.

'No, no, my dear. I mean every word I say.'

He glared at me defiantly.

'I know Mr Faraday will not agree, but I have never been more sincere.'

I shook my head.

'I'm not getting in the middle of this,' I said. 'When do we get to the meat?'

'After the soup,' the little old lady snapped in my ear. Ingolstadt and the girl laughed.

'You misunderstood Mr Faraday, Elvira,' he said gently.

His shrewd eyes turned back to me.

'I think we might wait until we reach the

dessert stage, Mr Faraday. My indigestion has been playing me up lately and I fancy I may find your news a little hard to stomach.'

'That's about right,' I said.

The soup was on the plates now and we started the meal. It was some of the best food I'd ever tasted and by the time the third course came up I was feeling a bit more human. Ingolstadt had been silent, concentrating on eating, but shrewd glances had been beaming from behind his gold-rimmed pince-nez at myself and the girl. His silver hair and his eyebrows looked more wind-blown than ever and he still wore the old dark suit with the loose fit and the same blue bow tie with white polka dots.

I'd finished the bourbon and was on my second glass of wine and warmth was coursing through me. I'd been thoroughly chilled earlier in the day but now the prospect was slightly improving. But only slightly. I hadn't forgotten what Ingolstadt had sent me into; and I didn't intend to. I had a lot of questions for him tonight and I wanted some answers before I left.

The old lady brought us the dessert and Ingolstadt got up and bustled about with a tray of liqueurs. His eyes gleamed from behind the glasses as he glanced at Elvira, who stood silently by the trolley, her beady little eyes matching his own for experienced cunning. I was suddenly aware that she was matching us drink for drink from her own supply at the edge of the trolley.

I guessed then she'd worked for Ingolstadt a good many years; that they thoroughly understood one another and that both could say exactly what they liked to the other without either taking offence. I'd come across such situations before. They're always a source of great amusement to outsiders and even with the hard core of anger smouldering within me, I could appreciate the flavour of the set-up.

'That was almost palatable, Elvira,' he said eventually, keeping his eyes fixed on her.

'Like your remarks,' she snapped.

'I don't deserve you,' Ingolstadt said placatingly, shooting an appealing glance at the girl and myself.

The old lady sniffed.

'We deserve each other,' she said enigmatically.

'I'm going to bed. I'll wash up in the morning.'

'Good night, Elvira,' Shelley Beeching said, giving the old maid an affectionate glance.

The woman's face softened as she looked at the girl.

'Good night, Miss Shelley. No doubt you'll be wanting to discuss private matters.'

She came up behind my chair and put a skinny claw on my shoulder.

'Be careful, Mr Faraday. He's more cunning than a wagon-load of monkeys.'

I grinned.

'I'll be careful. And thanks for the meal. It was great.'

The old woman's face was transformed.

'Here's someone at least who appreciates good food,' she told the shadowy ceiling.

'If there's anything else you need you'll have to get it yourselves.'

She clumped off aggressively toward the doorway. Old Ingolstadt chuckled to himself, looking after her affectionately. The door closed softly in a silence that was broken only by the low crackling of the fire.

'I think the world of that old woman, Mr Faraday,' Ingolstadt said. 'Though it wouldn't do to let her know.'

'You could have fooled me,' I said.

The old man got up and rooted around on the table.

'Let's take our coffee and drinks over by the fire. We'll be more comfortable there.'

We did like he said. I brought over the girl's cup and saucer and put that and her glass on a low table facing the fire. I slumped down in a leather wing chair near her while Ingolstadt remained standing by another chair at the opposite side of the hearth. His manner had undergone a dramatic change now that the old servant had left us. It was something he seemed to be able to do as easily as a costume artist changes his cloak on the stage.

I guessed it was all part of his persona as a

courtroom performer; all practising lawyers partake of the theatrical. It's in their make-up. He switched on a shaded lamp near the fire and went over and turned off the room-lights. I noticed that Shelley Beeching had gotten a small notebook from her handbag and sat with pencil poised, her eyes never leaving my face. I would have liked a smoke but I knew the old boy didn't approve.

Ingolstadt came to stand looking down at me in the lowered lighting given off by the single lamp and the fire.

'All right, Mr Faraday. I'll quit horsing around. Tell me everything that happened.'

CHAPTER SEVEN

1

The crackle of the fire seemed like an intrusion in the silence. Ingolstadt sat opposite, his brown face and white hair a startling contrast in the firelight. His face looked grim. Shelley Beeching licked the tip of her pencil with a pink tongue and stared thoughtfully at her expensive tan shoes.

'They were waiting for me,' I said. 'I'd like to know why.'

My anger was beginning to flare again.

'You knew what I was going into,' I said. 'You expected this.'

Ingolstadt shook his head.

'You can't say that, Mr Faraday. Besides, you haven't told me exactly what happened yet. I was testing out a theory.'

'An expensive theory,' I said. 'It got four men killed and I damn near got rubbed myself.'

I saw the shock on the girl's face and Ingolstadt looked at me as though I'd slapped him. His eyebrows were drawn-up in an incredulous line which furrowed his brow and made him look very old at that moment.

'You can't mean it, Mr Faraday!'

'I do mean it,' I said. 'And the police will want to know what happened. That means my head on the chopping-block. I had to open fire or they would have killed me.'

Ingolstadt waved his hand impatiently in the air.

'Never mind about the police, Mr Faraday. That can be squared all right, believe me.'

'I'm glad to hear you say so,' I said. 'Though I don't know exactly how.'

'You haven't told us the details yet,' the girl reminded me.

Her eyes were liquid with sympathy in the low-key lighting in here.

'I'll get to it,' I said.

'The whole thing was a come-on, wasn't it?'

I was addressing the lawyer now and I saw the professional pained look in his eyes; it

58

didn't fool me or throw me off.

'Let's level,' I said. 'I like to know what I'm getting into. You knew hitmen were trying for Sternwood or whoever tried to contact him. That was why you set me up with that phoney package.'

Ingolstadt shook his head. He was smiling a tight smile now.

'I didn't set you up, as you picturesquely put it, Mr Faraday. I was merely testing the strength of the enemy, which was why I warned you gun-stuff might be involved.'

'You can say that again,' I told him. 'It wasn't only gun-stuff. It was more like World War Two artillery-fire.'

I watched the soft flames of the fire dancing up the chimney.

'That address you gave me was phoney, wasn't it? There was nothing but a temporary sign stuck in the soil up there.'

Ingolstadt shook his head, the tight smile back on his face.

'There you exaggerate, Mr Faraday. Mr Sternwood is having a house built where I told you. Only it isn't yet finished. It seemed like a fairly good rendezvous to test out certain preconceived theories.'

'But it could have gotten me killed,' I persisted.

Ingolstadt vehemently shook his head again.

'If you'd gone on, Mr Faraday, there is a way out. The road loops around and keeps on

59

going. Otherwise, how could that second party of men have headed you off?'

'That's another thing,' I said. 'The whole play looked like a plan to knock me over.'

'Not you, Mr Faraday. They're trying to get Sternwood. Undoubtedly you were followed today. And it would have been easy for those men, if they knew the terrain, to send another party on the upper road to head you off. I had nothing to do with this whatsoever and no-one regrets more than I the danger to which you were subjected.'

'That was why the payment was so generous, wasn't it?' I said.

The girl bit her lip and kept her eyes on me, a troubled look on her face. Ingolstadt stroked his chin, his features heavy and brooding in the firelight.

'That was only a retainer, Mr Faraday. You will find me even more generous when the case is over.'

There was a long silence.

'That may be,' I said. 'But I'm going to find it difficult to collect if I'm dead.'

'You exaggerate, Mr Faraday. I am sure we will be able to take more adequate precautions in future, now that we are forewarned.'

'You're not out there on the street,' I said. 'Getting your underwear blown to lace.'

The girl was smiling now and even Ingolstadt opened his lips another four or five millimetres.

'There's a girl too,' I said. 'Sternwood's mistress, from what I hear.'

Ingolstadt laid his finger alongside his nose in an admonitory gesture.

'You got wind of that, did you?'

'Difficult not to,' I said. 'The papers were full of it a while back.'

'She is certainly concerned in the matter,' the old boy went on. 'I hope to go into that later.'

'You'll have to,' I said. 'If you want me to stay with the case. A rival faction is worried about Sternwood and his activities. I can see that all right. These things go on all the time in gang circles.'

Ingolstadt gave a heavy sigh.

'And in big business too,' I went on. 'If you insist on calling it something else.'

Ingolstadt interrupted me harshly.

'It is a little more complicated than that, Mr Faraday. I will certainly put you fully in the picture now that we know what we are up against. I must insist now that you tell me exactly what happened up there.'

2

There was another heavy silence.

'You asked for it,' I said.

I gave them a blow by blow description of what took place, Ingolstadt's expression getting grimmer with every second that passed.

Shelley Beeching gave a little catch of the breath when I got to the part where the automobile caught fire but her pencil went on racing across the paper without hesitation. She was a pro in her own field all right.

'You could not have got out without doing that?' Ingolstadt said at last.

He didn't say he was referring to the explosion and fire but he didn't have to.

'Of course I could,' I said. 'I could have gone into the woods and maybe starved; or broken a leg on the rocks and starved; or died of pneumonia eventually. I decided to survive. There were six of them, remember, maybe more. I wanted to create a diversion. They happened to get killed. That's the way it goes, sometimes.'

To my surprise Ingolstadt rubbed his hands.

'Oh, I am not criticizing, Mr Faraday. Merely getting at the facts. You have done excellently. Unless I miss my guess you have eliminated at least four of the most lethal hatchet-men in the whole of the L.A. basin. You are more likely to get a commendation from the Police Department than a reprimand.'

I looked at him dispassionately.

'That's good to know at least,' I said. 'Which also means you know who they were and what they represent.'

'I would never deny it, Mr Faraday. But this means a slight re-grouping of our resources

62

and a change in strategy.'

'You might let me know what he's talking about,' I told the girl. 'Or maybe you're wiser than I am.'

Shelley Beeching bit her lip.

'Please listen to Mr Ingolstadt, Mr Faraday. He is talking cold facts and you may take it from me there is nothing wrong in all this. You're on the right side.'

I stared at her moodily.

'That remains to be seen,' I said.

Ingolstadt got up from his chair.

'You have had a hard day, Mr Faraday,' he said cheerfully. 'Another drink will not come amiss? A bourbon this time?'

I nodded.

'I won't say no.'

I sat staring into the fire until he came back and put the glass in my hand. I was warm now and rested but I couldn't get out of my mind the car going up like a torch and the heat so tremendous that it blasted men even before they'd properly had time to scream. But, like I told Stella, it was them or me. And I was sitting here full of food and good liquor, being conned by one of the finest artists in the business.

'You still haven't told me anything,' I said.

Ingolstadt went to sit back in his armchair by the fire.

'Patience is not your strong suit, Mr Faraday.'

'So I've been told.'

I took a tentative sip of the bourbon and slightly swivelled in my chair so that I could see the old man better.

'Where is Sternwood? What is this stuff I'm supposed to deliver to him? And what has the girl to do with it?'

Ingolstadt's eyes were bright now.

'Ah, I can see you are interested again, Mr Faraday. All in good time. I must just think a few things through in the light of your new information.'

He picked up his own glass and sipped delicately at the contents, the firelight making brindled patterns on his mane of white hair.

'Jenny Holm is the young woman's name, Mr Faraday. You remember her?'

I sat back and closed my eyes. A face began to compose itself. A face that had been in every newspaper two or three years back. Sternwood's girl. The woman who had used a gun as savagely as a man, so the scandal sheets said, but who had never been convicted by the police of anything more serious than parking in front of a fireplug.

'I remember something about her,' I said. 'Something about her being a one-woman gang war. Suppose you enlighten me.'

Ingolstadt nodded, the firelight glinting on his golden-rimmed glasses and making him look like a benevolent grandfather such as used to appear in all those old Edmund Gwenn and Charles Coburn movies.

64

'I'll enlighten you, Mr Faraday. And when I've finished I'm sure you'll see the necessity for continuing with this matter.'

I nodded.

'All right, Mr Ingolstadt. But no more phoney packages. From now on I want to know what I'm carrying.'

Ingolstadt smiled slowly. He glanced from me to the girl and then back to me again.

'Very well, Mr Faraday. What I'm about to tell you is rather unusual and may go against the grain.'

I shot him a quizzical look.

'Against the grain?'

He shifted awkwardly in his chair, one hand round the stem of his glass.

'Against the grain from your point of view.'

'You'll have to be more specific, Mr Ingolstadt.'

'I intend to, young man, if you give me half a chance.'

He gave another of his irritating little smiles. Strangely, there was no trace of the clicking which I'd found so annoying on the phone. Maybe that was just one of his acquired mannerisms.

He was sitting upright in the chair now, his eyes fixed on mine.

'It's a strange story, Mr Faraday.'

I shrugged.

'I'm used to strange stories, Mr Ingolstadt.'

He shook his head warily.

'This is something a little different, Mr Faraday. A case of cry wolf. What would you say to the history of a man who is a gangster; a liar; a paranoic killer; and who has acknowledged more or less publicly to being the author of at least thirty killings?'

A bleak humour was sparkling in the old man's eyes now.

'There is a supreme irony in the situation, Mr Faraday. The irony of an innocent man, who may well face the supreme penalty for a murder he did not on this occasion, commit; a murder cooked up by his gangster and political rival Comstock. An innocent man who can only be saved by the testimony of Jenny Holm, herself a perverted liar and an acknowledged murderess.'

CHAPTER EIGHT

1

I didn't exactly whistle in the silence that followed but I certainly felt like it.

'You give me some nice cases, Mr Ingolstadt,' I said. 'But I'd appreciate you giving me a miss next time you're handing them out.'

Ingolstadt chuckled throatily, giving Shelley

Beeching a triumphant glance.

'You see, Shelley, just as I told you. This young man thrives on danger. I couldn't have got a finer representative in this matter.'

'You got the wrong word,' I told him. 'Sucker would be more appropriate.'

Ingolstadt chuckled again.

'You'll have to explain a whole lot more,' I went on.

'I intend to, young man, I intend to. And when I've finished, I'm convinced you'll see it my way.'

'I'll take a raincheck on it,' I said.

Ingolstadt clicked his teeth disapprovingly.

'You're a hard man, Mr Faraday.'

'That's how I survive,' I said.

I looked at Shelley Beeching's racing pencil.

'It's spelt with one v,' I told her.

She flushed and stopped writing. Old man Ingolstadt had been watching us with a crafty expression on his face.

'It's necessary to take such detailed notes, Mr Faraday.'

'I know,' I said. 'Just in case it comes to court later.'

He looked at me in genuine surprise.

'It'll come to court, Mr Faraday. Make no mistake about it.'

'Just make sure it's not me standing there,' I said.

He chuckled throatily.

'There's no fear of that, Mr Faraday.'

67

'Not from where you're sitting,' I said.

It was the girl who interrupted us this time.

'Gentlemen, please ...'

Her brown eyes were full of concern.

'I'm sure if you were in Mr Faraday's spot, Mr Ingolstadt, you'd want certain guarantees.'

The old boy pulled at the lobe of his ear and stared broodingly into the fire.

'You're right, my dear. It's just that I have to balance two considerations. My natural desire to put Mr Faraday fully in the picture and at the same time keep the professional confidences of my clients.'

I looked at him sharply.

'I thought you said client.'

He smiled crookedly.

'I was thinking of Sternwood and Miss Holm, Mr Faraday.'

I frowned at the old boy sitting there in the firelight, as cunning and knowledgeable as only experienced criminal lawyers can look.

'All right, Mr Ingolstadt, let's stop fencing,' I said. 'I'm open to persuasion. Just give me the story but make sure the facts are true this time. Sternwood is a businessman the same way I'm a teacher of sacred music.'

Ingolstadt smiled faintly at the girl.

'The facts were true last time, Mr Faraday.'

'Maybe,' I said. 'But you were just a little short on them.' He put the tips of his fingers together and examined them carefully, as though marshalling the details. It didn't inspire me with much confidence. Shelley Beeching moved uneasily in her chair, her brown eyes trying to warn me about something. I gave up trying to read them and concentrated on her general appearance as the silence went on.

She still wore the same outfit as when I'd seen her in the office that morning. So much had happened today it seemed like weeks ago. The gold chain and the ornament, a sort of plaque, which had engraved lettering on it, shimmered against her rust-coloured silk shirt as she moved under my scrutiny. She cleared her throat with a delicate sound.

'If you'd only stop criticizing, Mr Faraday, and listen carefully to what Mr Ingolstadt tells you, I'm sure we'll all get along much better.'

I grinned at her. The storm clouds were lifting now. And, after all, I was still in one piece.

'I'll give it a whirl,' I said.

2

'You're absolutely vital to this scheme, Mr Faraday. We can't do a thing without you.'

'What Mr Ingolstadt means is that we need you, Mr Faraday,' the girl said softly.

'If you put it like that ...' I said.

I still had the feeling I was being conned again.

'We do, Mr Faraday,' Ingolstadt said

69

earnestly.

'I'm not at liberty to give you all the details but I'll fill you in on the salient points.'

'I'm listening,' I said.

The old lawyer glanced moodily at the fire, the firelight flickering across his features, so that they looked faded and insubstantial in the dimness.

'What I'm going to tell you mustn't go outside this room.'

'Outside my office,' I said. 'I have no secrets from my secretary. We're like you and Miss Beeching here. I believe I mentioned it before. If not, I'm telling you now.'

Ingolstadt paused and shot me a displeased glance.

'Very well, Mr Faraday. The four of us, if you insist.'

'I do insist,' I said.

'As I already indicated,' the old man said, 'there's a gang war in progress. The opposition is out to get Sternwood. For your purposes his background doesn't matter. He's just my client. There's no doubt he's been framed on this occasion. You can take my word for it.'

I nodded without saying anything. The girl frowned at me and tapped with her pencil on very white teeth. The action reminded me vividly of Stella.

'Jenny Holm's evidence will at the least save him from a life term in gaol; at the most from a death-sentence.'

70

'You made your point,' I said. 'The opposition don't want the girl to appear. Don't want her alive at all, in fact. You got her under wraps, of course?'

Ingolstadt gave his eyebrows another airing.

'Of course,' he said ironically. 'That goes without saying.'

'So you want me to be a bodyguard as well?' I said.

The old man sighed.

'It is rather more delicate than that, Mr Faraday. Sternwood goes before a Grand Jury hearing in camera soon. We have kept the whole thing from the Press so far. Jenny Holm's evidence is vital to my client's defence. She is being brought from the East, but it has, naturally, proved impossible to keep all our intentions from Sternwood's rivals, notably the chief contender for his crown, Dan Comstock.'

I tossed the thing around in my mind. I still didn't like it but it was beginning to make sense now.

'When do I get to see Sternwood?' I said.

'You don't. Not for the moment, at any rate.'

'He's under wraps too,' I said.

'Naturally. We're bringing the girl from the East shortly. That's where you come in. You're to deliver her safely to a place where Sternwood's temporarily holed-up. Then your job's more or less done.'

71

'I'm looking forward to that,' I said. 'I'd still like one or two more answers.'

Ingolstadt shot the girl an exasperated look. 'Like what?'

'Like when the girl arrives. Where I meet her. Where I'm to take her. That will do for starters.'

Ingolstadt smiled faintly.

'Let me worry about all that, Mr Faraday. You'll be told in good time. Possibly even tomorrow. We're that close to it. The enemy forces will certainly be in disarray after today's debacle. It will be an excellent time to move.'

He certainly had a point there.

'Why don't the opposition simply knock Sternwood over?'

Ingolstadt shook his head.

'I was wondering when you were coming to that, Mr Faraday. It isn't so easy. Everyone is frightened of Sternwood and what he can do. He is surrounded by bodyguards and he lets only trusted people into his intimate circle.'

His eyes looked broodingly into the fire again.

'It's been tried before. It has only led to a cement overcoat and a convenient reservoir for the relevant hitmen on at least half a dozen occasions to my knowledge.'

I grinned.

'You're being honest about your client at last,' I said. 'Where's your justice now?'

'We're talking about the law, Mr Faraday,

not justice,' he said. 'They're two entirely different things.'

Ingolstadt looked annoyed, like I'd caught him off guard. I saw a glance pass between him and the girl.

'You are certainly correct on that score, Mr Faraday,' he said stiffly. 'But we are still under wraps as I pointed out earlier.'

'I won't forget,' I said.

There was a long silence.

'You can count me in,' I said at last.

Ingolstadt let out his breath with a satisfied sound.

'I knew I could rely on you, Mr Faraday. You won't regret it.'

'We'll see,' I said.

I got up. I suddenly felt tired. The girl gave me a sympathetic look. She got up too.

'I'll telephone you tomorrow,' Ingolstadt said. 'I hope you will give priority to this business above all your other commitments.'

'I'll be standing by,' I said.

He rubbed his hands.

'Excellent.'

The Beeching girl turned to her employer.

'I must be going too, Mr Ingolstadt. I'd like a word with Mr Faraday in private anyway.'

He glanced briefly at both of us.

'Very well. Please forgive me if I leave you to find your own way out. I'd appreciate it if you'd lock the door behind you, Shelley.'

'Of course, Mr Ingolstadt.'

73

I paused at the door as we went away. His white hair and intent face were still turned toward the fire like he could see things written there that were hidden to us.

CHAPTER NINE

1

We were standing in the porch before the girl spoke again. I'm six foot three but she was almost as tall as I was and I could see her face clearly in the gloom as she bent to lock the big door with a key she took from her handbag. The rain was still slamming down and cascading from the leaded roofs and gutters.

'That was a pretty good exhibition in there, Mr Faraday.'

I looked at her in surprise. Her face was set and there was a lot of frost in her voice. But she wore a white-belted raincoat with a sort of hood which framed her blonde hair and she looked so cute I couldn't summon up any more anger tonight.

'In what way, Miss Beeching?' I said evenly.

She shrugged.

'In many ways. Oh, sure, you had a reason after walking into danger like that, but you may rest assured that Mr Ingolstadt was just as shocked as I was. We didn't think they'd try anything on this early.'

'No?' I said. 'Which was why the old man provided the dummy packet instead of the important evidence he mentioned.'

The girl flushed. We were still standing in the porch and we'd moved under the brass lantern, which was lit.

'That was my idea, Mr Faraday,' she said in a low voice.

I grinned.

'I might have guessed. It was pretty smart at that because nine out of ten people would have been jumped.'

She looked at me with very clear and honest eyes.

'You weren't,' she said softly.

It was my turn to shrug.

'I'm the tenth,' I said. 'Shall we sit in my car or yours?'

She looked at me swiftly.

'Yours,' she said.

We went down the steps together. I hadn't locked my heap but even so the rain was so heavy we were thoroughly damp before we'd tumbled inside. I thought of something then.

'Where's your car?'

'Round the side in the garage. There's an entrance from there into the house.'

'I'll bet there is,' I said. 'I'll drive you round.'

I fired the motor and idled the Buick along the vast bulk of the house, the yellow headlights slicing across soaked shrubbery and rain-streaked windows. We glided past a vast glass-house which appeared to be full of exotic plants.

'He should have called this Wuthering Heights,' I said.

The girl smiled. She looked beautiful like that. There was no other expression for it.

'Just here, Mr Faraday. Underneath the arch.'

The drive dipped and curved here. I hadn't come in this way so I'd no idea of the scale of the place. We drove under an ornamental stone bridge on classical lines that soared into the air, spanning the roadway and linking the higher part of the garden with the house and garage. At the bottom of the road we drove under an arch into peace and quietness. The big double doors of what appeared to be a bus-depot were open and in the dim interior light bulbs burned in metal wall fittings. There were two or three vehicles in there; I guessed the gleaming Packard belonged to the girl.

I killed the motor and we sat for a few moments.

'What do you think about all this?' I said.

She shrugged non-committally.

'I'm just Mr Ingolstadt's hired help, Mr Faraday. It's not my function to question his doings.'

'Oh, come on,' I said. 'It's me you're talking to. You're his right-hand. He said so himself.

It's my bet you know more about his business affairs than he does himself.'

The girl smiled again.

'You flatter me, Mr Faraday.'

'I don't think so, Miss Beeching.'

She looked at me seriously.

'If you want long and detailed answers to awkward questions, Mr Faraday, I can't give them to you.'

I frowned.

'So you've got no advice to give me at all?'

She shook her head.

'I didn't say that. My advice would be the same as before. Just trust Mr Ingolstadt. That's all I have to say.'

I nodded.

'Let's leave it at that. I trust you at any rate.'

'That's something, at least. But if you trust me, you trust Mr Ingolstadt.'

'We'll see,' I said. 'But thanks for the advice.'

'I hope you take it,' she said quietly.

She slid out the car with a quick, supple movement. She leaned back in to offer me a warm, brown hand to shake.

'Thank you for the lift, Mr Faraday. You'll be hearing from us.'

'Sure,' I said. 'See you.'

She ran into the gloom of the interior. I re-started the Buick and went on a little farther to turn around. When I drove back there was no sign of her and her car hadn't appeared. I wondered whether she'd gone back into the house again to report to the old boy.

Anyway, it was no business of mine. I got the hell out and drove carefully back over to my rented house on Park West. I ran a shower and dumped my mud-stained clothing, found a fresh outfit for the morning. I looked even worse than I figured in the bathroom mirror.

By the time I came out I was almost asleep on my feet. I went around and made sure the place was secure, flipped off all the lights and got back up to my bedroom. I was asleep as soon as I hit the pillow.

2

I struggled out from under layers of mush at the strident urgency of the telephone bell. It was still dark in the room so I put on my bedside lamp, was blinded by the glare. While I groped for the phone I glanced at my watch. I swore. It was all of four a.m.

'Faraday? This is Ingolstadt here.'

'Nice to hear from you,' I said. 'I always get bored during the dead hours between midnight and eight a.m.'

The teeth-clicking routine started again.

'I hope I didn't get you out of bed.'

'Of course not,' I said. 'What would I be doing wasting my time sleeping at four a.m.?'

'Well, I'm sorry about that, but I warned you you'd have to earn the money. I want you

78

to listen carefully and memorize what I'm going to tell you.'

'You'll have to wait a minute,' I said.

I put the phone down on the table, got out of bed and went out to the bathroom. I ran a tap over my head, towelled myself down and was wide awake. I went back and sat in a cane chair and picked up the telephone.

'No notes,' Ingolstadt said warningly. 'Memorize what I'm going to tell you and then repeat it, so's we're sure we understand one another.'

'I'm listening,' I said.

'Something broke,' he said. 'We think this would be a good opportunity. Jenny Holm's flying out. Her plane arrives at L.A. International at seven a.m. this morning. That's in three hours' time.'

'That's great,' I said. 'It means I can have another leisurely hour's sleep before I hit the road.'

'It can't be helped,' he went on imperturbably.

He was an amazing old boy. Somehow, I gained the impression that he hadn't been to bed at all yet. Though maybe he was one of those old characters who need only about three or four hours' sleep a night.

'She's registered in the name of Chalmers,' Ingolstadt went on.

'Got it,' I said. 'I'll be wearing a white rose up my right nostril so she'll recognize me.'

Ingolstadt clicked his teeth again.

'Spare me the humour, Mr Faraday,' he said. 'This is serious. I think that's about all.'

'Just a minute,' I said. 'Where do we meet? And, more important still, where are we going? Not to mention the 5,000 dollar topper. How do we avoid getting shot at by the opposition mob?'

'That's been taken care of,' Ingolstadt said. 'I've got some help at the airport in case you need any assistance. But they won't bother you that time of the morning. The trouble will come the other end, when you take her to meet Sternwood.'

'I'm glad you mentioned that,' I said. 'And are we using my car?'

'The girl knows all that,' Ingolstadt said patiently. 'You'll be using a hired Cadillac in the name of Smith.'

'Original,' I said.

Ingolstadt ignored that too.

'Leave your car in one of the Airport carparks for a day or two. The girl knows where you're going and she'll give you your instructions.'

'Like hell she will,' I said.

Ingolstadt's tones were patient.

'I thought you were going along with this, Faraday. Believe me, it's all been very carefully thought out.'

'If you say so,' I said. 'After all, you're picking up the tab. And you'll pick up the tab if anything goes wrong and I lose her.'

'You won't lose her, Mr Faraday, if you play ball,' he went on. 'I realize you're not used to being closely supervised like this but we're up against a desperate mob. It'll work out.'

'I hope you're right,' I said.

I was getting one of my premonitions again. It must have been something to do with the hour. I repeated all the stuff he'd told me and he expressed satisfaction with the state of my memory.

'Is there any objection to letting me know where the girl's coming from?' I said. 'Or is that restricted information too? Just so that I can be at the right gate to meet her.'

'Of course not, Mr Faraday,' he said. 'My apologies. It's the New York flight, arriving at 7.05 a.m. Mrs Chalmers will be wearing black and carrying the current issue of *Cosmopolitan*. She's supposed to be arriving for a funeral.'

I gave a heavy sigh.

'It figures,' I said.

I heard the click as the phone went down. I looked at the clock. It wasn't worthwhile going back to bed. I padded downstairs to brew myself some coffee.

CHAPTER TEN

1

I was on the road just before six a.m. but traffic was heavy even at that time of the morning and it had turned twenty past by the time I hit the freeway. It was still raining nicely and the slurry thrown up by vehicles in front made a fine soupy mixture on the windshield.

I got out there by six forty-five a.m. and checked in. By the time I'd parked and found out it was Gate 12 I wanted I was already beat. I pounded back down and got in position just on seven a.m. I needn't have bothered anyway, because it was seven thirty-five before the flight showed.

The Smith-Wesson in its nylon webbing harness felt a little more bulky than usual. I'd put three spare clips in today, just in case. If last night was anything to go by I might be needing them before the day was out. There still hadn't been anything on the radio about the shoot-out. And I'd glanced at the early editions at a bookstall while I was waiting without finding even a stick on the subject. I figured Dan Comstock's people had taken care of the matter.

The big jet was taxi-ing now, its motors

kicking up sheets of spray from the tarmac. I sighed. Clearance would take a little while still, especially if the airport authorities had ordered any baggage checks for suspected terrorist activity. The aircraft was wheeling away while I thought about this. It glided up the apron and out of sight. I kicked my heels for a while longer, idly looking at the people clustered in front of me, waiting to greet their nearest and dearest.

I went back a way from the gate and found a phone-booth. There was quite a queue but I got in in the end, keeping a sharp eye on Gate 12. There was no sign of the aircraft or the passengers. I quickly dialled Stella at her apartment. She came on straight away so I guessed she must have been up already.

'My,' she said. 'The dawn chorus.'

'Never mind the cracks,' I said. 'I'm at L.A. International.'

I could feel Stella's surprise all the way from where she was sitting.

'I haven't got much time,' I said. 'Got a pencil?'

I waited a few seconds while she fetched some paper. She took notes as I spoke, without making comments. I could see the tip of the aircraft's wing now, working back up toward Gate 12.

'You sure you told me everything, Mike?' Stella said when I'd finished.

'Everything of importance,' I said.

Stella let out her breath in a little explosion of sound.

'Looks like you won't be around for a while,' she said.

'Looks like it,' I said. 'Mrs Chalmers, to give you her assumed name, is calling the shots from now on. I'll be in touch when I can.'

'Let me hear from you,' Stella said. 'And be careful.'

I chuckled.

'You know me, honey. Anything after yesterday would be anti-climax.'

Stella's voice was so low I could hardly hear it as she said goodbye. I put down the phone and got out the booth in a hurry. The big plane was clearly in view, the engines still going, water rippling in sheets on the runway. I relinquished the booth to an excitable fellow with a thin smear of what appeared to be cotton wool under his nostrils and walked back over toward Gate 12.

There was quite a crowd of people waiting for the plane to arrive now. We stood there for perhaps five minutes with nothing happening at all. Then the engines cut out and one could hear again. Another ten minutes went by while we watched the sheeting rain starring the puddles. This was great fun. And to think you could have been wasting your time at home in bed now, Mike, I told myself.

I eased forward a little. A dark stream of figures appeared around a corner of the airport buildings. They were coming off. I worked my way a little farther forward through the crowd, keeping my eyes sharply peeled. I couldn't see anyone suspicious around. But then I wouldn't expect to. Mobsters specialized in ordinary-looking hitmen who wore anonymous clothes and had anonymous sorts of faces.

I presumed they would be from Comstock's mob; Ingolstadt had hinted at it. Or at least a combine of Sternwood's political and mob rivals with Comstock's men. I had to play this carefully if I was to stay in one piece. And there was another handicap in that I had apparently to take instructions from Jenny Holm, who knew a great deal more than I did about the set-up. I didn't like it at all.

I appreciated the old boy's comment about the law being different from justice, but I liked to be on the right side in my cases; I'd have preferred to let the two factions slug it out. And then there was another complication; the men Ingolstadt said would be at the airport to give us assistance and create a diversion if necessary.

I wondered where he'd got them from. Perhaps employed another firm of private eyes; or some professional sluggers wily old lawyers like him often took on to their pay-rolls. I hoped there wouldn't be any need for diversions today. Life was too snarled-up already.

The leading passengers in the file were

85

almost up to the gate. Most of them appeared to be on package tours, judging by the U.S. flag labels many of them had pinned to their lapels. There was a good sprinkling of grim-looking mauve-rinsed matrons, and a few obvious salesmen laden with briefcases and executive bags, carrying journals devoted to computer technology. They were in their early forties and all had prematurely aged faces, with heavy bags under the eyes.

Then I saw the girl I wanted. I didn't need to look at the magazine she carried. She was in the middle of one of the biggest parties and trying to be as unobtrusive as possible, but she was so good-looking she still stood out. Which was a distinct disadvantage from my point of view. I stood to one side and took a sharp look around me. There were too many people for anyone to try anything here.

The girl was tall and slim; with a classical line to her body that was only emphasized by the tight-fitting, well-cut black tailored suit she wore. She had on black, high-heeled shoes and her blonde hair gleamed with drops of moisture under the small black hat. It had a sort of black scarf attached to it which looped round her face like a coif, leaving her left-hand cheek covered.

She carried a small brown dressing-case in her right hand and a white raincoat over her left, with the issue of *Cosmopolitan* clutched against the coat. She went straight through the gate without hesitating and I followed on quickly behind. She half-turned as I got to her elbow, giving me a hesitant smile.

'Mrs Chalmers?' I said. 'I'm here to meet you as arranged.'

She handed me the case to carry, putting up her hand to mine.

'Mr Smith, of course. Let's go to the car-park. We haven't much time.'

2

She threaded her way through the crowds without speaking and I almost had a job to keep up with her. I kept a sharp look-out and stationed myself on her right so that I could keep my right hand free for the Smith-Wesson if necessary. To do that I shifted her case to my left. It was so light she could have had little in it. I couldn't see much of her profile, because it was partly hidden by the scarf or whatever you called it.

We were down by Gate 15 now, the thunder of engines filling the air and she turned back toward the car-parks, like she knew the airport intimately. She probably did, come to that. I kept my mouth shut and concentrated on searching the faces of the crowds round about us. I felt exposed and vulnerable here. In the noise and confusion anyone could chance a shot without people being aware of it.

The same thought must have occurred to the girl because she suddenly said to me over her shoulder, 'It isn't far now, Mr Faraday. The sooner we're under way the better.'

'Suits me,' I said.

She nodded, handing me a set of car-keys on a small leather label-holder. She was looking around her sharply, as though searching carefully for something. I realized she wasn't worried about being followed but orientating herself on the domestic features of the airport. Then she moved sideways, walking purposefully, looking at the metal numbers of the parking aisles.

'This must be it,' she said, indicating a dark brown Cadillac that bore the stencil of a well-known L.A. hire-firm on the door-panel. As I bent to unlock the driver's door I caught sight of the licence details round the steering post. There was a card jammed in the top which bore in large crayoned letters: Mr Roderick Smith. The usual documents that one gets when renting a car were lying on top of the instrument panel.

I grinned.

'You thought of everything.'

The girl shook her head, giving me a tight smile.

'Not me, Mr Smith. The organization.'

'Oh, yes,' I said. 'The organization. I'd forgotten.'

I turned to look round the parking-lot.

88

There was no-one sitting in any of the automobiles parked in this section.

'Will you drive or shall I?'

The girl shook her head.

'You drive, Mr Faraday. I'll tell you where.'

'Fair enough,' I said.

I put the girl's overnight case down on the back seat, leaned over to unlock the door. She was round the other side almost before I'd completed the motion. She slammed the door behind her, sitting with compressed, tight features looking to the front. Seen this way, I was getting her left-hand profile; the obscured one. She kept her hat on and the scarf arrangement draped across. She gave a bleak smile as she caught my glance.

'You wonder why I wear this outfit, Mr Faraday. I have to now. Permanently.'

'I don't understand,' I said.

She shook her head.

'You will. It covers a scar. It was given to me by one of Sternwood's boys. By way of a warning.'

She shivered suddenly and I felt a faint stir of pity.

'I'm sorry,' I said. And meant it.

'Don't be,' she said. 'I knew what I was getting into.'

She opened a handbag she carried and got out a pack of cigarettes. She lit one and sat forward, staring through the windscreen, puffing furiously as though to erase an unpleasant memory.

I started up the motor and eased the big car gently out the parking slot, making sure I cleared the two tightly parked vehicles either side. The girl's eyes were stabbing every which way and I knew she'd give me ample warning if she saw anything suspicious. I eased forward, glad of the power-steering and tooled on down between the ranks of parked vehicles, the rain falling steadily and monotonously all the time, though it was nothing to what it had been the previous day. The Caddy was much bigger than the Buick and I had to watch my clearances.

The girl had had her raincoat over her shoulders while we were coming through the car-park, but now she slid it off, folded it and threw it over on to the seat behind. Like everything she did, her motions were economical and purposeful. I looked at her covertly as we drifted slowly on toward the nearest entrance, getting in a long queue of vehicles that were going that way.

She was about twenty-eight, I should have said, and had a smooth, unblemished face. The hat and the dark scarf under her chin covered most of her hair but what I could see was a burnished blonde. She had a wide, generous mouth; good teeth and dimples at the corners of the mouth. The nose was retroussé; the chin strong and resolute. She had me puzzled. She wasn't what I had expected at all.

There was nothing brassy or cheap about her; and her voice was low and cultured. Her whole manner, in fact, was quiet and discreet beyond what one would have expected, given her situation. Yet I was thinking in clichés. The days had long gone when gangsters' molls were recruited from the lower echelons. Mobsters nowadays were more likely to run to college graduates with Ph.D.s to their name. There's no justice, Mike, I told myself.

The girl must have sensed something of my puzzlement for she smiled gently. It altered her face completely, making her mourning outfit look momentarily ridiculous.

'I'm not what you think, Mr Faraday? You were expecting someone entirely different?'

'Maybe,' I said somewhat uncomfortably. 'Maybe not. I don't know what I expected, really.'

I turned to look at her briefly in the eye. I liked what I saw. The eyes were pale green and very steady.

'You've got guts, I'll give you that,' I said. 'I wouldn't want to be in your shoes, Mrs Chalmers.'

She puffed absently on the cigarette, then took it out of her mouth.

'Thank you for sticking to my nom-de-plume at least, Mr Faraday. But I understand you've already been in my shoes, if I read Mr Ingolstadt correctly.'

'You do,' I said grimly. 'You can thank him

for my being here. If I had a grain of sense I'd have been home eating breakfast now.'

The girl smiled again and took another puff of the cigarette, holding it between two fingers like a child might when trying her first smoke. All the while her eyes were scanning the other vehicles in the queue, people walking on the airport road, the windows of buildings about. Everything was half-hidden now in the increasing veils of rain.

The car in front suddenly braked and I pulled up with a slam. I had the Smith-Wesson halfway out the holster when I saw the little black automatic at the mouth of the Holm number's bag. Our eyes met ironically.

'Your reflexes are good, Mr Smith,' she said, closing the bag as the car in front crawled forward again.

'So are yours,' I said. 'Your reputation hasn't been exaggerated.'

'I hope yours hasn't,' she said with exaggerated politeness, looking beyond me at vehicles tailing back the other way. We were up to the entrance gate now and I pulled the big car over, waiting for a slot in the traffic on the slip road.

'Any reason I shouldn't know where we're going?' I said.

She shook her head.

'All in good time. Just drive the way we're going, if you please.'

I bit back my curiosity, put in the gear and

idled out into the traffic stream.

CHAPTER ELEVEN

1

It took me more than half an hour to get clear of the main traffic stream. I chose a side road after a bit and lost most of the heavy stuff. Then, at the girl's direction, I turned the Cadillac north, snaking up into the foothills which were blurred now with the driving rain and hemmed in by black clouds that seemed to come down to meet the faint mist that was rising. It made for lousy driving conditions but it suited my situation because it was that much more difficult for the opposition to find us, stay with us or knock us over for that matter.

And I especially didn't want them to knock us over. The girl had been quiet until we cleared the city and even now she didn't relax, turning to crane out through the rear window and looking carefully at every car that came from the opposite direction on the narrow mountain roads.

'What's our routine, if that's not a top-secret too?' I said at last.

The girl smiled faintly.

'We're Mr and Mrs Roderick Smith now for

Mr Ingolstadt's purposes. We're going to hole up somewhere for the night. In two separate rooms, in case you're getting any ideas.'

I stared thoughtfully at the girl's silken legs; the black skirt had ridden up with the motion of the car. She grinned and put her hand on her knee.

'What makes you think that, Mrs Chalmers?' I said.

The girl shook her head impatiently.

'Mrs Smith,' she corrected me. 'You're no different to any other man, Mr Faraday.'

'Mr Smith,' I said. 'We won't be very convincing as a married couple if you're going to call me Faraday all the time.'

She bit her lip and anger flickered momentarily in her eyes.

'I'm sorry,' she said quietly after a moment. 'It won't happen again, Roderick.'

'That's fine, Jenny,' I said.

I turned the Cadillac at an intersection and took the road which still led upward. We drove up into the hills for several hours, with the houses getting scarcer all the time. I hoped we wouldn't meet anyone from the opposition up here. I'd already had enough of that the previous day. And with a woman, it might be too much of a handicap. Though from what I'd heard of Jenny Holm and her prowess with a gun, we could give a good account of ourselves.

But even so the odds might be too great this time. They wouldn't miss out on the second occasion. And I wanted to collect that extra bonus Ingolstadt had been talking about. Not that I'm mercenary. But if I went out on this assignment it would provide something for Stella. I grinned to myself. I was beginning to think like an old married man making his will. I resisted the image of Stella and pushed it to the back of my mind.

I remembered then I'd asked her to give me a rundown on Sternwood; by the time I saw her again the whole case would probably be over. And I'd have heard from Sternwood personally what the score was. If we got through to him. I became conscious of the girl's eye on me. She was certainly a cool one. She was behaving as though we were on a honeymoon trip instead of a couple of hunted fugitives.

Her situation was more desperate than my own. I was a hired gun. I could opt out at any time. But she was a marked woman in every sense of the word. They'd be on to her if I was here or not. I was coming to revise my opinion of her with every minute that passed. I'd be openly admiring her if I went on like this. I glanced at my watch as we changed direction again, still going upward.

'I hope we can get something to eat where we're going,' I said. 'It's nearly lunch-time.'

She smiled thinly.

'Don't worry, Roderick. We're almost there.'

The rain was coming down in almost vertical sheets now. I sighed. It looked like we were in for weeks of this. The only cheering thing in prospect was lunch. One lived from hour to hour on this sort of assignment. Not that I'd had many. I didn't want many like this, even for what Ingolstadt was paying.

I remembered my new outfit which had been ruined yesterday. I upped the expense account Ingolstadt had mentioned by another fifty dollars. I felt better then. I turned back to the girl.

'Any objection to telling me where we're going, now?'

She shook her head.

'Not at all. As I said, we'll be there in a few minutes. It's a place called the Mercador Motel. It's fairly big, with plenty of people staying there, even this time of year. We can merge with the background.'

'So can the opposition,' I said.

The girl put her chin out defiantly.

'You can leave me to look out for them, Roderick. I can smell one of Comstock's mob a mile off.'

'You may have to,' I said. 'We're going to find hotel life pretty inhibiting up here, especially in this weather.'

The blonde girl shook her head again.

'We shan't be here long enough. Like Mr Ingolstadt said the real danger will be when we get close to Sternwood.'

'Tell me about him,' I said.

'Not now, Mr Smith,' she said gently. 'Perhaps when I get to know you a little better.'

I nodded, looking through the smeared windshield. A big white-painted sign was coming up at the roadside. It spelled out: MERCADOR MOTEL.

2

The Mercador, when we got there, proved to be very impressive indeed. The entrance was divided into two sections, one leading directly into the motel complex; the other into a small private filling-station run by the company. I turned the Cadillac into the right-hand forecourt. This automobile was very heavy on gas and the tank, which had been full when we'd started from L.A. International, was already below the halfway mark if the gauge was correct.

Jenny Holm looked at me approvingly but said nothing, puffing nervously on a cigarette. There was no-one at the gas-station but a slim, dark girl in a white slicker came scampering across the tarmac from a glassed-in office at the motel reception building opposite. She shook the flecks of water from her long hair and smiled brightly in my open driving window as she came under the canopy.

'Some weather.'

'Fill her up,' I said.

The girl nodded and went over to the pump. She came back over while the fuel was going in.

'You staying here?'

'Just for the night,' I said.

'I can put the gas on your bill if you'd rather. All right for oil and air?'

'Fine,' I said. 'It's just been checked.'

The girl smiled again. It may have been my imagination but it seemed to me like she was looking at us with more than ordinary curiosity.

'Many people in this time of year?' I said.

The girl looked enthusiastic.

'Pretty full. It's the heated swim-pool and the other facilities that bring them. Maybe I'll see you around the pool tonight.'

The question was addressed to me solely, not to both of us and I noticed Jenny Holm's smile from the corner of my eye.

'Maybe,' I said. 'I'll take a raincheck on it.'

The girl smiled softly, her eyes flickering to the pump dial across the forecourt.

'Raincheck's right,' she said.

I paid her and added something for herself. She was running across beneath the thick streamers of rain before I'd turned on the motor. I eased the Cadillac back across the tarmac and down the short driveway edged with tailored stone-walls which had richly coloured tropical flowers growing from the interstices.

The girl was already in position behind the desk of the office before I'd pulled up under a big glass canopy that kept off the rain. MM, the cipher of the Mercador Motel, was over the big swing doors and let into about every pane of glass that I could see.

Jenny Holm got out and I handed her her minuscule grip. She stood looking at me with a mocking expression on her face. I got out my raincoat and handed hers out too. I looked at her uncomfortably.

'I forgot something,' I said.

She shook her head.

'It's all been taken care of. Just open up the boot.'

I did like she said, walking around and avoiding the puddles where the heavy rain had drifted under the canopy. There was a very expensive-looking leather suitcase sitting in there. It had the initials R. S. in metal let into the leather. I noticed then that she had her own initials J. S. on both her handbag and the small case she carried.

'Ingolstadt thinks of everything, doesn't he?' I said. 'You planned this trip a long time ago. You'd already started on your flight west long before the old man called me this morning.'

'Of course,' she said calmly. 'The less anyone knew about the trip beforehand the better.'

I hefted the bag out and closed the boot.

'I'll bet the old man chose the contents of this as well,' I said. 'Even down to the mauve

99

pyjamas.'

The girl smiled, standing there under the canopy, watching me patiently like she was an ordinary wife on an ordinary trip with her husband.

'He has far more taste than that, Roderick. But he didn't choose the stuff on this occasion, though I'm sure you'll find everything you'll need. We're only staying the one night, you'll be pleased to know.'

I grinned.

'Depends on how tonight goes.'

The Holm number rolled a very pink tongue around her mouth.

'Don't get your hopes too high,' she said dryly.

I tested the boot, made sure it was locked.

'Just for your information, Shelley Beeching chose that stuff.'

I put my head on one side, looked at her reflectively.

'In that case I do have something to look forward to this evening,' I said.

We went in through the big swing-doors to where the dark girl sat patiently waiting for us.

CHAPTER TWELVE

1

She'd taken off the slicker to reveal a pretty sensational exterior. What she had was covered by a tan open-neck shirt and matching tan trousers but the material underneath was pretty firm and pneumatic in all the right places. She smiled as we got up close, revealing very white teeth.

'My uncle owns this spread,' she said. 'It isn't worth our while employing a gas-attendant.'

'I'm sure the clients prefer you,' I said gallantly.

I looked beyond her desk to the vast glass wall where fountains played in a plaza glowing with light. There were faint shrieks and splashes as people dived into the heart-shaped pool. Up above a band was playing somewhere and I could see the tables of a large restaurant through the banks of tropical greenery.

'Some spread,' I said.

'We like it,' she said. 'We have some two hundred cabins dotted around a hundred acres of landscaped woodland.'

'You needn't go on,' I said. 'I'm already impressed.'

The girl gurgled to herself, looking from me to the Holm number questioningly.

'Would you register, please. I've given you Cabin No. 48. It's only a hundred yards off so you won't have far to come for meals in this weather.'

'Sounds fine,' I said.

'I'll fill it in, dear,' the blonde number said

101

before I could add anything else.

'Mr and Mrs Roderick Smith of San Francisco.'

She put her handbag down with the initials prominently displayed. The girl behind the desk caught sight of it, like she was meant to. It stifled any doubts she might have had in her mind. I could see that from her eyes. She looked at me in what I could have sworn was a disappointed manner. She waited impassively while Jenny Holm filled in the card. She'd obviously got everything pre-arranged with old man Ingolstadt because she filled everything in without hesitation, in a firm, bold hand.

The girl took the card and held it under her desk lamp so she could read the details.

'Fine. Here's the keys. The doors are automatic, Mr Smith, so you just drive straight in. Make sure you don't miss the metal strips, though.'

'Sure,' I said. 'I saw Laurel and Hardy do that once.'

The girl laughed. Jenny Holm stood watching the two of us, one hand on her hip, like she was a spectator at a play.

'I'm afraid we brought our baggage in,' I said. 'I thought the rooms were in here.'

The dark number put up her hand and patted a lank strand of hair into place on her dark head.

'That's all right. I'll take them out for you again.'

She strode round the desk with lithe steps and picked up the two cases before Jenny Holm and I could say anything. She was already out under the canopy before I got to the doors. The blonde girl had a familiar glint in her eye.

'If you want to make your own arrangements for tonight, don't mind me,' she said.

I grinned.

'I'll take another raincheck,' I said. 'I have my own duties to attend to.'

The dark girl turned round, her face flushed.

'I'm Sylvia Ashton,' she said. 'Your hostess, as it were. You'll be eating in the restaurant, I take it?'

'You bet,' I said. 'Lunch and dinner. We'll be over for the first in half an hour.'

The girl stood and watched us as I got in the driving seat. She opened the passenger door for Jenny Holm and slammed it behind her. Another car was coming up through the mist and the rain by then and Sylvia Ashton got the white slicker from a peg near the big swing doors and sprinted over toward the gas-station as I tooled the Caddy on out.

'A lively little thing,' I said.

Jenny Holm grinned.

'If you like that sort of stuff,' she said. 'I

prefer men around six feet tall with jaws like granite.'

'I should just about suit, then,' I told her.

We were gliding down a red asphalt road between shaved lawns now and I concentrated on the steering, looking for the cabin numbers that were coming up on white boards on posts set in the turf.

'Any other time, Mr Faraday,' she said softly. 'This is strictly business.'

'I know how it is,' I said. 'I feel the same way myself.'

Just then I saw the number 48 come up to the right and turned the wheel quickly, conscious of the pressure of the Smith-Wesson in the nylon holster against my chest muscles. I did like the girl said, aiming for the two metal strips set in the tarmac apron in front of the big double garage doors. They slid up and over and a bulb winked on in the interior. I drove on in feeling like I was going into a coffin.

2

I lit a cigarette and looked round the room with satisfaction. It was a nice set-up, with panelled walls and twin beds with a table and shaded lamp between. I went back and got the bags from the garage, found the lever that controlled the doors. I left the Caddy to dry out and came back in, locking the cabin door

104

behind me with the key that was already in the lock.

I put it down on the bedside table.

'So we'll know where to find it in a hurry,' I said.

The Holm number had taken her raincoat off and now she looked at me thoughtfully. It was difficult to talk in here because the rain was drumming heavily at the windows. I went over and drew the louvred blinds. The room lights came on as Jenny Holm got to the button.

'Why not leave the key in the door?' she said.

I shook my head.

'And have someone surprise us? Supposing they came through the garage while we were asleep. They could put a sheet of paper under the door and work the key out.'

Jenny Holm smiled.

'You've been seeing too many Edwardian movies. They'd be more likely to use a skeleton key.'

'Maybe,' I said. 'But I'm a light sleeper and would probably hear anyway. Safer to have the key out the lock.'

'Just as you wish. You're in charge of security.'

'Just so long as you remember that,' I said.

I went through into the next room. That was got up as a day-lounge with a big divan, a colour TV set and a telephone like the bedroom. I went through the far door. There was a small entrance hall leading to the front door. I prowled round the cabin for a while, watched by the Holm number. It was solidly built of local stone, with thick walls and cedar shingles on the roof. It was about thirty yards from its nearest neighbour and had outside lights that could be worked from the hall.

'Seems pretty satisfactory,' I said.

'That's why Mr Ingolstadt chose it,' the blonde girl said.

She kept the scarf arrangement around her face, even while we were indoors.

'If you want to use the bathroom, I'll wait,' I said. 'I don't want to be too late for lunch.'

'You won't be,' the girl said. 'Just give me three minutes.'

She disappeared. I knocked off the ash from my cigarette in a tray near the bed and unpacked my case. That didn't take long. If Shelley Beeching had packed the stuff, she was a pretty good guesser. The pyjamas were a dark red, with the white initials R. S. worked on the breast-pocket; they were just about my size.

For the rest there was a towelling robe; a water-proof bag which contained soap, a razor and shaving gear; a couple of hand-towels and some after-shave lotion. I carried the robe and pyjamas over to the right-hand bed. The Holm girl came back and watched me. I grinned back at her over my shoulder.

'Just set-dressing. I'll be using the divan in the other room for tonight.'

The girl nodded.

106

'Mr Ingolstadt's ringing in tonight to confirm our destination for tomorrow.'

'The master-planner,' I said.

I looked round the bedroom, hefted my case up on to the wooden rack at the bottom of the bed.

'There's a locking door between the two rooms,' I said. 'For obvious reasons we'd better leave it open tonight. And I don't want you to misunderstand me.'

The girl shook her head.

'I don't misunderstand you, Mr Faraday. And I entirely agree. But if you have to come in in a hurry just make sure you announce yourself properly. I'll be sleeping with the pistol under my pillow.'

'Sure,' I said. 'So long as we both know the drill.'

I went over and flipped off the bedside light. 'Now, let's eat.'

CHAPTER THIRTEEN

1

It was still raining. From the restaurant table I could see clear over the Mercador complex and it wouldn't have been possible to have found a wetter piece of real estate outside Venice. The

107

small orchestra was doing its best to infuse some gaiety into the proceedings and a concealed projector was showing Technicolor scenes of Hawaii on to a screen outside fake windows that made it like we were in the tropics. It was all right if you liked that sort of thing. I happened to be in the mood for it today.

The food was excellent and we'd both done justice to it. I'd had only a couple of cups of coffee and some toast for breakfast due to my early start and I hadn't realized how hungry I was until I'd sat down. Ingolstadt had one good idea in choosing the Mercador; I had to give him that. Everything about the place, given the outsize style of California, was done with taste and wit, given the premise that they wanted to entertain the customers under one roof when the weather was wet like now.

I glanced over at the girl. She still wore the scarf arrangement, but somehow it looked appropriate here, like it was a once fashionable style that was coming back in again. Come to think of it, it had been fashionable in forties movies. I recalled people like Judith Anderson and Gene Tierney carrying it off with great élan. We are being fancy, Mike, I told myself.

The girl's eyes were searching the room with quiet persistence all the time we were eating.

'Anything?' I said.

She shook her head.

'Perhaps. Perhaps not.'

I glanced round the big restaurant.

'I can't see anything suspicious.'

The girl lowered her eyes to the plate again.

'You don't know Dan Comstock. He employs some extraordinarily innocuous-looking people.'

'Like yourself, for instance.'

Jenny Holm's face took on an expression of distaste.

'I walked into that one. But it's true. You don't know him. If you did you wouldn't sit here so calmly.'

'Perhaps it's because I'm so calm that it helps the façade,' I said.

The blonde number nodded.

'I'm sorry,' she said. 'You stung me for a moment. And that doesn't often happen. You don't like people like Sternwood either, do you?'

'Does anyone?' I said. 'Decent people, that is?'

The girl looked at me curiously, her fork poised in one hand, her face dimly profiled against one of the big picture windows streaming with rain.

'You're a strangely mediaeval man, Roderick.'

I was glad to see she was keeping up the façade.

'What does that mean?' I said.

She shrugged.

'You have this weird concept about people.

People aren't simple, they're very complicated. You see everything in black and white, whereas it's every shade of grey.'

I grinned.

'I found that out a long time ago, Jenny. It's just that maybe I'm prejudiced. I operate at the gritty end. I'm usually the one who's clobbered by the sort of operations people like Sternwood and Comstock mount.'

She looked at me with a curling lip.

'No-one asked you to become a private dick. It's your own crusade.'

'I take your point,' I said.

I picked up my glass of lager and looked moodily into its clouded surface.

'Anyway, we're in this together now. We've got to trust each other. We might as well be friends.'

The girl's expression had changed.

'We are friends, Roderick,' she said. 'It's just your high moral attitudes that stick in my craw.'

I gave her a long look.

'Maybe neither of us knows the other,' I said. 'There just isn't time on an assignment like this. And we're getting off the point.'

'You're right,' she said. 'We're just working together. Best to leave it like that.'

The waitress in the pink gingham was bringing our coffee now. It was that sort of place. A familiar figure was threading its way through the tables below the balcony on which

110

we were sitting. There would have been a spectacular view from here if it hadn't been for the rain and the mist. An appealing face looked up at us.

'Hi! Having fun.'

'Sort of,' I said. 'Come and join us.'

Jenny Holm smiled and reached out for the silver-plated sugar bowl on the table in front of her.

Sylvia Ashton came up the curving teak staircase to the balcony with long, easy strides. She paused by the table, looking down at us with mischievous eyes. She still wore the same outfit as when she'd been in the office but she looked better-groomed somehow.

'Comfortable in the cabin?'

'Fine,' I said. 'Sit down and have some coffee.'

'If Mrs Smith doesn't object.'

'Why should I object?' Jenny Holm said dryly. 'We've been married for years and you should know how married people get when they're cooped up together in a strange place and it's raining.'

I tried to look offended but the two women only laughed the harder. The Ashton number sat down and one of the waitresses was suddenly at her side with a spare cup and saucer. She turned to look at me intently.

'No, I don't know, Mrs Smith. How is it, Mr Smith?'

'So-so,' I said non-committally.

The two girls seemed to be enjoying all this more than I was.

'We're having a sort of water-gala tonight,' the girl said absently.

'Very appropriate,' I said.

She looked at me ingenuously.

'I thought you might like to join in.'

'Too strenuous,' I said. 'But we'll gladly watch if we've got time.'

I reached over for the silver pot and poured the girl some coffee. Jenny Holm sat and watched us in silence, her eyes wary and alert as her gaze wandered over the tables about us. I noticed she had her handbag open on her lap in front of her. Once again I gave her full marks for professionalism. There wasn't much chance of us being jumped with her around. She was really doing my job for me. Which meant there was something wrong somewhere.

The Ashton girl was leaning toward me now. She spoke in a low voice.

'If you don't mind me saying so, Mr Smith, your wife's a remarkable woman.'

I grinned over at Jenny Holm, who was looking away from the table, her thoughts evidently far from our small-talk.

'In what way?' I said.

The girl glanced back over her shoulder.

'Difficult to pin it down,' she said. 'But she's a person of quality.'

'I give you that,' I said, but I was still puzzling out Sylvia Ashton's words as we

pounded over the wet tarmac back to Cabin 48
and they stayed with me all afternoon.

2

'Your call, I believe, Roderick.'

I blinked at the Holm girl. Blue spirals of
smoke were rising toward the ceiling of the
cabin and the rain was splashing heavily at the
eaves. It had long been dark and the lights
outside our cabin were illuminating the
shimmering strips of concrete in front; the
zigzag path that ran down from the main door
and the apron in front of the garage section.
There was an exterior lamp over the double
garage doors and I'd got that on as well.

That way we could see if anyone was coming
a long way off. There were street lamps on the
internal roads as well and they'd been lit some
while.

The doors to the cabin were locked and
chained and we'd got the heavy curtains
drawn; barring accident I figured we were
pretty safe for the time being. It was the sheer
monotony of the job that was getting me down.
The Holm girl had read earlier in the afternoon
and when she did talk she'd refused to be
drawn about aspects of Ingolstadt's
assignment. Other than that she'd got evidence
that could save Sternwood; that I already knew
of course. I'd suggested cards after and we'd

been playing two-handed stud since four o'clock in the afternoon.

I stubbed out my cigarette in the tray on the table and looked at my watch. It was getting on for eight o'clock. I threw down my cards. The girl sat watching me with wide eyes.

'Let's call it a day,' I said. 'It'll be time to go back up for dinner soon.'

Jenny Holm smiled. She had a sort of calmness about her that was beginning to get on my nerves. Usually potential witnesses in murder trials, especially those who've been threatened by a mob, can't stick the sight of their own shadow. But this one was different. And it worried me. Sure, Ingolstadt had told me she had nerves of steel, but Jenny Holm didn't tie up with any preconceived ideas I'd had about the set-up.

The words Sylvia Ashton had used earlier in the day kept coming back into my mind.

'She's a person of quality,' she'd said.

It was true and it stuck out. She wasn't anything like a gangster's girl and it bugged me. Not because it had upset all my notions. It ran deeper than that. I kicked it around in my mind for a while longer. I looked across the table at Jenny Holm again. She had a sort of serene repose about her that I'd seen in few women. She could be silent too and there was a kind of ease about the quiet that didn't call for any effort on the part of the person she was with. That was a rare quality in men, let alone women. You're becoming a male chauvinist pig, Mike, I told myself.

The girl put her hands together primly in her lap, the table lamp shimmering on the blonde strands of hair.

'You don't think we should give dinner a miss this evening? Perhaps have a tray sent over?'

I shook my head.

'There's no reason to believe anyone knows we're here. So far as our real identities are concerned, of course. But if anyone is waiting around to jump us, having trays sent over would be an ideal opportunity. I'd rather go to them than have them come to us. They'll find it a lot more difficult in a public restaurant.'

'As you wish, Mr Smith,' she said softly. 'You may be right. We'll play it your way.'

'When are you contacting Ingolstadt?' I said.

The girl shook her head.

'He's ringing us. I thought I told you that. There's no way of knowing when.'

I stubbed out my cigarette butt in the tray and sat back, locking my hands behind my head. I could feel the comforting pressure of the Smith-Wesson against my chest.

'Supposing he rings when we're at dinner?'

She shook her head again.

'It won't matter. He'll be sure to phone back.'

'You seem to know him pretty well,' I said.

115

She put up her hand suddenly to adjust some strands of hair that were straggling from behind the scarf.

'I know Ingolstadt, sure. I knew him in the old days when I was with Sternwood. I was there when they had a number of confidential talks.'

'What's Sternwood like?' I said.

'I think you already asked me that too, Mr Faraday.'

It was the first time in some hours she'd used my proper name and she bit her lip. I didn't say anything and she went on after a moment or two.

'I will tell you this. He's surprising also. Just as you had certain fixed ideas about me, I think you'll find him entirely different to what you think.'

I got up and stared down at her as she sat in the chair. I could see the gleam of the pistol in the half-open neck of the handbag she had at her side.

'Why are you going to bat for him now, after what he did to you?'

She looked at me coolly, stubbing her own cigarette in the tray. She suddenly seemed conscious of the expanse of thigh she was showing because she smoothed down the stocking over her knee and stood up with a swift movement.

'You find that strange too, of course?'

'Not normal,' I said.

116

She had an odd look about the mouth as she stared at me in silence.

'You know very little about women, Mr Smith.'

'So I've been told, Mrs Smith,' I said.

'Just because a relationship has been terminated it doesn't mean that aspects of it don't linger on. There are some things about the past you can't forget. If I've been wronged I owe Sternwood certain favours too. That's why I'm coming along for this ride. To pay a debt, if you like.'

I stared at her in silence for a moment.

'You may find it a high price, Miss Holm.'

'Since we're dropping aliases for the moment, Mr Faraday, it's one I'm prepared to pay. But you don't have to stay.'

I shook my head and stood back from the table.

'I've been bought and paid for.'

She smiled faintly like she approved of my remark.

'There's nothing more to be said, then.'

She turned on her heel.

'I'll just get ready.'

She walked over toward the bathroom and a few moments later I heard the tap running. She'd left the door wide open and I had a strange hunch then. I walked on over, my footsteps muffled on the thick carpeting. I eased round the door lintel. Jenny Holm had taken off her scarf and had been sponging her

117

face with her flannel. She was bent over the basin, reaching for a towel.

I could see all of her features reflected in the big square mirror screwed to the tiling in front of her. She was a beautiful woman. More important still there was no sign of a scar on her left cheek.

I had a lot to think about as we walked up to the restaurant ten minutes later.

CHAPTER FOURTEEN

1

A streak of scarlet arced downward, entering the green water of the pool with scarcely a ripple, the flames from the cardboard hoop flickering brightly before they went out. The orchestra broke into a chord and a smatter of applause from round the pool-side was taken up by the diners in the restaurant. The dinner was as good as the lunch and the water gala was all right too.

Jenny Holm sat sideways on to me at the edge of the balcony. We'd slewed our chairs so that we could eat and watch at the same time. We were a bit exposed up here and at first I'd had second thoughts about sitting at the balcony edge. But there was plate glass

118

separating the restaurant from the pool area and anyone trying a shot would have not only the heavy glass, which might well deflect a bullet, but the reflections of hundreds of lights to contend with.

You're becoming an hysterical old woman on this case, Mike, I'd told myself. I'd already pointed out to the girl not once but half a dozen times that there was no reason for anyone to know we were here. But I'd begun to realize the problems endemic to the life of a fugitive. There was nothing tangible about it; it was just an enervating, will-sapping strain; the necessity to be alert at all times, which could all too easily lead to fear.

I glanced over at the girl. She'd just been applauding but all the time her eyes were ceaselessly raking over the people down below at the pool-side; the fellow-diners in the restaurant; and the waitresses passing and re-passing on their various errands. I almost wished we'd taken her advice and dined in the cabin. But there had been a lot of commonsense in what I'd told her. And we'd have died of boredom for sure back there.

I'd pushed the question of the scar on the girl's face to the back of my mind; or rather the question of there being no scar. It was only a flash, it was true, and it may have been an optical illusion caused by the bathroom lighting but I didn't think so. The girl hadn't seen me and I'd quietly withdrawn to the bedroom where I'd picked up our raincoats.

If she had no scar, why had she lied about Sternwood's boys disfiguring her? Or perhaps she'd had plastic surgery and was still sensitive about a slight disfigurement? I shoved it all back for the evening. I had enough problems as it was and the additional brainwork was spoiling my concentration.

I turned my eyes away from the next act, two girls in scarlet bikinis and two muscular young men who were about to attempt something back-breaking from the high boards. The Holm girl was interested in the gala now so I kept my eyes peeled. There was absolutely nothing out of the normal. A few middle-aged couples near us; a sprinkling of obvious newly-weds, who were holding hands under the table; a party of fifteen who looked like visiting Elks or Rotarians at a table farther down the balcony.

They all wore plastic buttons and slightly glazed looks; the women with the obligatory blue-rinsed hair and with the name-buttons on their evening gowns; while now and then they rent the air with what appeared to be slogans or communal jokes. I glanced down along the tables at the edge of the pool in the patio below. The waitresses and the male employees of the Mercador were equally obviously what they appeared to be.

There was another burst of applause and I focused again on Jenny Holm, who was

120

clapping like she meant it. The water slopped heavily against the sides of the pool with the shock waves of the multiple high-dive. The girl gave me a tight-lipped smile.

'This must be a bore for you.'

I shook my head.

'Not a bore. Something more than that. A blankness and a deadness with something deadly at the centre.'

Jenny Holm opened her eyes wide.

'You should have been a poet.'

I grinned.

'I have to make my own amusements on my cases.'

The girl looked serious. She glanced down at the half-open mouth of her handbag.

'You must have a lonely life.'

'At times. The job has its compensations. Like now, for example.'

She smiled gently again.

'Yes, you couldn't call this boring. And the food really is excellent.'

'I hope Ingolstadt is paying,' I said.

The girl waved her hand to indicate the restaurant and the swim-pool complex below.

'For everything, Roderick. Put every last nickel down on the tab.'

'I'll do that,' I promised her. 'But I don't like working in the dark.'

'You can't pick and choose if you want to make money,' she said crisply. 'I've found that out in my life.'

121

'And have you made money?' I said.

She shook her head.

'That would be telling, Mr Smith.'

Heads were turning around us and there was another smattering of applause. Bare feet vibrated on the carpet. A generous quantity of bronzed flesh split by scarlet erupted into view. A bare brown arm came round my neck and drops of moisture descended on me. The girl's breath was warm in my ear.

'How did you like our display?' Sylvia Ashton said.

2

I gently disengaged myself. The girl was dazzling all right.

'I like the display fine,' I said.

Sylvia Ashton shook her dark hair, sending drops of crystal scattering over the carpet. It was so warm in here her body was almost dry already. Jenny Holm smiled at me conspiratorially. The girl slid into a chair opposite, putting a white towelling wrap around her shoulders. I was conscious of the glances of the people at the tables round about. Too conscious. This was a spotlight we could have done without.

'Oh, was that you up there?' Jenny Holm said. 'It was just great.'

'Tremendous,' I said.

Sylvia Ashton flushed and reached out for the glass I pushed toward her. There seemed to be a lot of spare stuff on our table this evening. I poured her a glass of white wine and she cupped her hands around it, leaving it untasted.

'That's very kind of you both.'

'You have a talent,' I said.

The girl shrugged her brown shoulders.

'It's the wrong sort,' she said. 'I'm no good at academic things, that's the trouble.'

'No trouble,' I said. 'With what you've got who needs academics.'

'Gallantly put,' said Jenny Holm ironically.

'If you'd like me to leave, I'm quite willing,' she went on. 'The best part of the gala seems to be over.'

'It's just begun,' I said, looking pointedly at the Ashton girl's bikini.

She took a sip of her wine, looking uncertainly from one to the other of us.

'Take no notice of me, Miss Ashton,' Jenny Holm said. 'I was horsing around to relieve the monotony.'

The girl in the red bikini looked disappointed.

'And we thought we'd got something pretty good going at the Mercador.'

'You have,' I told her. 'In every way. It's just the weather. It's fine in here. It's when you get outside.'

'Maybe we should have covered rampways

123

to the cabins,' Sylvia Ashton said.

She sounded quite serious.

The waitress came up with coffee at that point and the girl took the opportunity to excuse herself.

'Thanks for the wine,' she said brightly. 'Maybe I'll see you later on. We have dancing from eleven o'clock.'

'Maybe,' I said.

I watched the girl run lithely down the staircase and through the lower restaurant. A few moments later a scarlet streak arced into the pool beyond the big plate-glass windows and creamed effortlessly across the water. The girl seemed as keen and eager as a puppy; there was something appealing about her. Apart from the obvious attractions, of course. But beneath it there appeared to be a kind of loneliness. Maybe it was just because she stayed put in one place at the Mercador and the world and its excitement, represented by the guests, passed by all the time.

'What it is to be young,' Jenny Holm said mockingly.

I lit a cigarette and reached out for my coffee cup.

'You should know,' I said. 'There can't be more than a couple of years between you.'

The girl shook her head, putting her cup back with a faint clatter that sounded clearly over the noises of the restaurant.

'There's all the world between us.'

'You said it,' I told her.

She didn't speak again until we left the restaurant. I looked back once and saw Sylvia Ashton come down again from the high board. She dived cleanly and entered the water with hardly a ripple. Not for the first time I regretted my assignment. I could have stayed up here a few days longer and I wouldn't even have noticed the weather.

We turned across the broad acres of shaved lawn and concrete pathways, shining and cold beneath the light of the overhead lamps. I had the Smith-Wesson and held it ready under the spread folds of my raincoat which I'd got hanging from my shoulders. The girl walked close at my side, in the shadowy section, away from the lamps. She'd taken up that position without being asked; she had the finest instinct of self-preservation I'd ever seen in a woman.

It was turned ten o'clock when we reached the cabin and I went on ahead, buttoning the lights. Everything was normal but I went right through the place just to make sure. The girl stood in the hallway while I did that and I could hear her locking and chaining the main door. We left the outside lights on. When all that was over I went in the bathroom, dried my hair on a towel and washed my hands. When I came out it was all of ten-fifteen. We had a long night ahead of us.

'You think Ingolstadt phoned?' I asked Jenny Holm.

She sat in a deep chair near the divan in the living-room, smoking and holding her head on one side like she was listening for things I couldn't hear above the battering of the rain.

'We'll know soon enough,' she said. 'Excuse me. I think I left that issue of *Cosmopolitan* in the car.'

I sat down on the divan and lit a cigarette while she went on out to the bedroom to fetch the key and unlock the door. I watched the lit rectangle that led to the garage and listened to the rat-tatting of her heels. I put the spent match-stalk in the tray on the table and listened to the rain. There wasn't much else to do up here this time of night. Apart from the radio. And a few obvious things if Jenny Holm and I had been married.

I put that out of my mind. She was taking a long time. I was just about to get up when she came back, rather hurriedly, an apologetic smile on her face. She buttoned the light and closed the door behind her. She was about to re-lock it when I interrupted her.

'You can leave that,' I said. 'I'll take a last look-around before we turn in.'

She hesitated, her hand on the door-knob.

'As you wish. It's rather foolish of me, actually. I seem to have left that magazine in the bedroom after all.'

I looked at her blankly. I'd already seen her put it down on the bed-side table when we'd first arrived. And she must have seen it when she went to get the key. That's why I'd asked her to leave the door unlocked.

She hung around for a minute or two, finished off her cigarette.

'I'll go wash-up,' she said. 'We'll give Ingolstadt till midnight.'

'Fine,' I said. 'I'll be right here.'

I waited until I heard the key turn in the bathroom lock. Then I padded on quietly over to the door that led to the garage. I opened it and buttoned the light. At first sight I couldn't see anything. My brain must have been made of marshmallow this evening. We'd been walking back through mud and water and neither of us had bothered much about wiping our shoes when we came in. One doesn't when living in rented hotel accommodation. A sad fact but true.

But the girl had still been wearing her raincoat when we'd come in. It was pretty wet and had been dripping water. It had left a small trail. She'd gone along the side of the Caddy like she'd been looking through the windows on to the rear seats for that issue of *Cosmopolitan*. I still didn't see it for a moment or two. But the play about the magazine had been an obvious lie and I'd got that missing scar on her face to think about.

Then I noticed where water had dripped from the skirts of her raincoat down on to the concrete floor. A little pool had gathered near the rear tyre. And next to it there were some scrapings of mud that had obviously come from her shoe. I got it then. She'd knelt down near the bodywork. But for what purpose? I looked around quickly. Then I pussyfooted back to the bathroom door. I could hear water running and the girl vigorously scrubbing her teeth.

I went back in the garage, got down at the rear of the Caddy. The floor was too wet and muddy for me to lie down and I couldn't clean up because I would have needed the bathroom for that. So I had to compromise. I got out my pencil-flash and went over the chassis. I didn't see anything. Then I reached under the sill of the bodywork, where it curved up over the rear wheel. I felt a small metal disc which slid along.

I pulled it off. It didn't want to come because it was magnetic. When I got it in the palm of my hand I recognized it. It was one of those small electronic bugs that police agencies and espionage outfits use to keep track of moving vehicles. There was no doubt in my mind the girl had just put it there. I looked at it again to make sure but it just sat there in the palm of my hand looking bland and innocent. I replaced it carefully, making sure it was in the approximate position I'd found it.

I was smoking a second cigarette, my mind heavy with thought, when Jenny Holm came out the bathroom. The shrilling of the telephone bell in the silence of the cabin seared my nerves like acid.

128

CHAPTER FIFTEEN

1

The girl was over to the table-phone before I could move.

'Mrs Smith? Yes, this is she.'

She turned to me, cupping the receiver.

'Ingolstadt.'

I went to stand at her side.

'Everything's just fine, father. No, no, all went well. Roderick is here with me now.'

I grinned crookedly, my shadow thrown huge on the wall by the lamp on the table.

'Give him my love, dear.'

She ignored that.

'Yes, I understand,' she went on. 'First thing in the morning.'

'Can't he make it late afternoon,' I said. 'All this early stuff isn't in my contract.'

Jenny Holm smiled, though she turned her back in order to concentrate on what Ingolstadt was saying.

'By dark,' she said. 'Yes, we can make it all right. We've gassed up here and if we take something to eat with us, we may not have to stop.'

She went on in that way for another ten minutes or so. I gathered old man Ingolstadt was giving her details of our route for the morning. I stood and smoked and pulled what was left of my mind together. It wasn't so very hard to do. Everything was in pieces and nothing fitted except that we were probably going into a shooting gallery if Ingolstadt hadn't got the action plotted right. Shelley Beeching seemed to have a lot of confidence in him. I wished I could have said the same. Jenny Holm finished at last and handed the phone over to me.

'Are you there, Mr Smith?'

'Just about, uncle,' I said. 'I gather we're making an early start again tomorrow.'

'I'm afraid that's it,' he said in his jovial way.

I waited for the teeth-clicking routine but he didn't seem to be in the mood this evening.

'Miss Beeching sends her regards.'

'Give her mine,' I told him. 'I'd like you to get a message to Stella if you would.'

'To what effect?' he said cautiously.

'Just tell her we're fine,' I said.

I could feel his apprehension disappearing even though we were way off at the other end of the line.

'Will do,' he said briskly. 'Now, Mr Smith, I want you to listen carefully. We've succeeded so far because we've been extremely cautious and proceeded step by step. Tomorrow will be the critical day and we must carry on in the same manner.'

'I take it we get to meet our client then,' I

said.

He did click his teeth at that point.

'That is approximately correct,' he said. 'Because of that we must take special precautions.'

'Meaning what?'

'You'll find out in good time,' he said. 'For your own protection I've given Mrs Smith map co-ordinates. You'll have to follow the instructions pretty carefully.'

I stared across the shadowy motel cabin to Jenny Holm's enigmatic features. She was sitting back underneath the table-lamp now, picking a fleck of tobacco off her pink tongue and following every syllable of the conversation.

'Map co-ordinates?' I said. 'What is this. An O.S.S. operation?'

'Very necessary, Mr Smith, I can assure you,' Ingolstadt went on patiently.

'But we'd need special maps for stuff like that,' I objected.

Ingolstadt gave a heavy sigh.

'But you have them, Mr Smith, you have them. Your wife has a special large-scale. She has just memorized the co-ordinates. That way, if you're intercepted or separated, it will be an additional safeguard.'

'For Sternwood?' I said.

'For everyone,' he said smoothly. 'Well, I think that is about everything, except to wish you luck.'

'We could do with plenty of that,' I said.

There was a hollow click at the other end of the line. I put the receiver back in the cradle and walked over to where Jenny Holm sat.

'You heard all that?'

'More or less.'

'It doesn't make sense,' I said. 'The whole thing's screwy.'

She shook her head patiently.

'It does make sense, Mr Smith. You'll see when we get up there.'

I sat down in a chair opposite and stared at her.

'You begin to sound more and more like Shelley Beeching,' I told her. 'Just what is it this old man's got that makes young girls eat out of his hand?'

She laughed, showing very good teeth, pushing back the scarf a little from her smooth features.

'Something that young men seldom have, Mr Smith. Wisdom and patience. It appeals to young women a good deal.'

'It must do,' I said. 'Are you going to leave me those co-ordinates? Just in case you forget them?'

She shook her head again.

'No point for the moment, Roderick. I'll let you know tomorrow. I have the details firmly in my head, don't worry.'

'All right,' I said.

I stood up.

'I have to leave you for half an hour.'

'Why?'

'Because I'd better go settle the bill with the Ashton number and get some sandwiches, coffee and stuff for the journey tomorrow.'

The girl nodded.

'I'll be fine.'

The small pistol from her bag just melted into her hand.

'Don't be longer than half an hour.'

'I won't,' I said. 'I'll give three straight knocks on my return.'

I turned at the door. She was already on her feet, coming across the room toward me.

'We're still heading north?' I said.

'Correct,' she said. 'Still heading north.'

I heard the bolts and chain go on behind me before I got a yard down the cement path.

2

I sat upright on the divan and looked at my watch. It was three a.m. and my tray was full of crushed cigarette-butts. It was one hell of a way to spend the night but things had been too quiet so far. I'd decided to bunk down fully-dressed on the divan, with just the small shaded lamp, and keep watch. The Smith-Wesson was lying on the table next me and I had an extra sandwich in a plastic wrapper in case I felt hungry in the night.

Jenny Holm had gone to bed before midnight but she'd kept the door open like we'd agreed. I hadn't gone near the bedroom in all that time and I hadn't heard any sound from her so I guessed she was asleep.

I got up and went over to the bathroom and ran a tap over my head. I rinsed out the tooth-mug and drank a little of the water. I felt slightly better then. My face looked back at me, sardonic and dark-eyed from the mirror. I went back to the living-room, switching off the light. I had a half-bottle of bourbon, bought from the hotel bar earlier in the evening, and I poured a small shot into the glass. It took away the taste of the water.

Rain was still rattling on the roof like it was never going to stop, though it wasn't as brutal as it had been. The only good thing about it was that it reduced visibility and would make us harder to spot on our way northward tomorrow. Where? That was the question. It was only one of a number rattling around in my brain-box for the moment. I was convinced now that Jenny Holm was playing a double-game. I could have been mistaken about the scar, sure. The lighting was dim in the bathroom and plastic surgery could have removed most of the damage caused by Sternwood's boys.

And she may have been sensitive about her looks, like most women. I understand that all right. But there was a far deeper question,

134

posed by the electronic bug fixed underneath the Caddy. That had more sinister implications. Our movements were being monitored, that was for sure. Or would be, in the morning, unless I removed it. The girl might have been acting on Ingolstadt's instructions. Or not. Just who was monitoring our movements was the big question-mark that was interesting me.

And if I moved the bug I might well be endangering us if Ingolstadt had ordered it put there. The only other possibility was that Jenny Holm was playing her own game. But on whose behalf? There wouldn't be much point if she was doing it for Sternwood. He already knew about the situation and Ingolstadt was working for him anyway. Presumably he knew where we were coming from and what the score was. That left the question of Dan Comstock and his mob.

It was a big question but it was unbelievable that the Holm girl could be leading the gang to Sternwood. Though it was a possibility. I'd given up trying to figure the female mind years ago. As hatred was close to love so love was close to hatred. Maybe Jenny Holm's insides were still festering over that scarring; the wound to her love, her pride and her looks.

I gave a heavy sigh and lit another cigarette. I was leaning forward to put the match in the tray on the table when I became aware that I wasn't alone. Jenny Holm was watching me

135

from the shadows of the bedroom doorway. She wore a white dressing gown made of some shimmering material which looked quite fetching. She still wore the scarf arrangement and that looked fetching too. There were dark stains under her eyes though. I guessed that like me, she hadn't been able to sleep.

'I left my cigarettes on the table,' she said.

I nodded. I pushed back my blanket, got up and offered her the package. I lit her cigarette from the end of my own and she stood there, looking at me with big eyes and drawing in the smoke gratefully. She put the package in the pocket of her dressing gown.

'I've been thinking,' I said. 'This early start of ours. Won't it cause more suspicion than otherwise? If we stayed to breakfast like normal tourists...'

She shook her head, her eyes still searching my face.

'It isn't that, Mr Faraday. We could easily stay for breakfast. There's little real danger to be expected here. But we've got to allow a lot of time tomorrow.'

I sat down on the divan again and looked at the half-inch of bourbon in the bottom of my glass.

'What for?'

'Not for the distance. But we've got to do a lot of doubling about and re-tracing our route. Until we're sure we've shaken Comstock off.'

'If he's ever been on our trail,' I said.

136

The girl gave a cynical smile.

'He's been on our trail all right, Mr Faraday. You can be sure of that.'

'Mr Smith,' I said. 'I take it you and Ingolstadt know what you're doing.'

'This is no game,' she said. 'And my neck's in more danger than yours. So we'll play it my way.'

'I'm not arguing,' I said. 'I've played it your way so far.'

'Yes, you've been good,' she said mockingly.

I leaned forward to pick up the glass. I drained the last of the bourbon in it. I looked at the bottle.

'You want one?'

She shook her head.

'Not this time of the morning.'

'You have the map?' I said.

'It's here, Mr Faraday.'

She took it out one of the deep pockets of her dressing gown.

'You're welcome to look at it. But it won't tell you anything. I have a plastic cover sheet in my luggage, which gives the co-ordinates. You have to use the two together.'

I expelled a long plume of blue smoke and watched it slowly ascend to the shadowy ceiling.

'Thanks for nothing,' I said.

She laughed. It made a hollow tinkling sound above the rain.

'You'll find out everything soon enough, Mr

Faraday. Then maybe you won't like it.'

'We'll see,' I said.

She didn't say goodnight, just melted back through the open bedroom doorway.

'Goodnight,' I told the empty room.

I got back up on the divan again, pulled the blanket round me, locked my hands behind my head and listened to the pattering of the rain. Stella's face was the last thing I saw before I drifted off to a broken sleep. It was one hell of a way to spend the night.

CHAPTER SIXTEEN

1

It was around 4.30 a.m. when the shrilling of the phone brought me out of my doze. My mouth felt like it was full of cornflakes. I got over to the phone in two seconds flat. It was only the operator to tell me it was 4.30 a.m. I thanked her and put the instrument down. I hadn't doubted her. It felt like 4.30 a.m. too. The rain was still falling softly on the roof.

I buttoned the main room lights and went over toward the bedroom but the Holm number was already moving around.

'All right, Mr Faraday. Please use the bathroom first if you want to shave.'

I did like she said. I hadn't had many advantages on this case and this looked like one of them. My face looked a wreck in the mirror and my hair stood up like Stan Laurel's. I ran some hot water and made with the stuff Shelley Beeching had provided. In twenty minutes I re-emerged from the ordeal feeling more like a human being. But one never feels right sleeping in one's clothes. I went through into the garage while the girl used the bathroom.

The place smelt cold and damp and full of stale air. The Caddy was icy-cold to the touch and there was the sharp tang of oil and gasoline in the atmosphere. I went back in the living-room, got the suitcase and re-packed the stuff. I put the receipt from the Mercador in my bill-fold. By the time I'd done that the girl had gone through into the bedroom, slamming the door behind her.

I sat down and lit my first cigarette of the day. If you discounted the half-dozen or so I'd smoked since midnight. Then I noticed the bourbon bottle, re-opened the case and put that in. I got the Smith-Wesson from the table and put it back in my shoulder-holster. I felt almost ready to face the day by the time I'd tasted a cup of coffee from the thermos pack that had been provided with the Caddy. Ingolstadt—or Shelley Beeching—seemed to have thought of everything.

The girl was back in the room now. She was

139

fully dressed and looked as fresh as though she'd had fifteen hours' sleep.

'You want coffee?' I said.

She shook her head.

'It's time to be moving. I'll have some once we're on the road.'

She went restlessly round the room, making sure she'd left nothing. She carried her raincoat over her arm. She started to put it on and as I went to help her she moved away.

'I can manage.'

'Suit yourself,' I said.

I went out in the garage and buttoned the light. There was a small circular window up front. I looked through. Nothing moved in the radiance of the lamps set along the ribbons of tarmac that stretched away in the rain. I went back and got my case. I shoved it on the back seat. Jenny Holm was out with me now, carrying her own small holdall. She put it down on the back seat too. It may have been my imagination but her face looked cold and strained in the harsh lighting.

'You want to drive or shall I?' I said.

She shook her head.

'You drive. I'll do the navigating.'

I noticed then she'd got the large-scale map. It was folded in four and she kept it in her hand. She went back through into the living-room and I followed. I checked the bathroom but I couldn't see anything there that belonged to me. I got the tooth-mug from the table and

140

rinsed it in the bathroom wash-basin before putting it back in the cupboard. Then I folded the blanket I'd used on the divan, straightened the cushions and went into the bedroom to put the blanket back on the rack at the end of the bed.

Either Jenny Holm hadn't used the bed or she'd straightened it already because the coverlets looked immaculate. I went back in the living-room and looked round carefully, my mind heavy with thought. I stubbed out my cigarette in the tray on the table, then took the tray out and flushed its contents down the toilet. Nothing like being careful. The girl was out at the car again by now. Probably checking that the bug was still in place. I saw my lips tighten in the bathroom mirror.

Then I went in the living-room for the last time, got the flask and the sandwiches and took them out to the car. My first cup of coffee was percolating through my system nicely by now and I felt a little more human. The girl was standing near the bonnet of the Caddy, looking out through the circular window. I went to stand by the rear wheel, where the bug was, leaning casually against the bodywork. I kicked the rear tyre, like I was checking the pressure. My foot slipped on to the bodywork, making a hollow metallic noise. Jenny Holm bit her lip and started forward.

'We'd better get moving, Mr Faraday.'

'You already said that,' I told her. 'I'm ready

141

when you are.'

She looked at me as though she was about to say something, then bit the words back. She went round to the passenger seat. She put her handbag down on the squab. Like always, the mouth of it was open. She still carried the folded map in her right hand.

'What about the doors?'

'They operate in reverse, from a ramp inside going out,' I said. 'Just get aboard.'

She did like I said and closed the door with a heavy click. I got in and fired the motor. It sounded like Hiroshima inside this confined space. But I guessed none of the people sleeping in the cabins round about would have heard it. I wished now I'd reversed the Caddy in the previous night. If there was anyone around at this hour of the morning we'd be sitting ducks with me having to go out like this.

The girl evidently thought so too because she had the pistol out now. She held it loosely in her right hand, keeping the map in her left. She'd put the handbag somewhere down at her feet. I reversed slowly toward the big up and over doors. I felt the rear tyres on the ramp and then the doors slid up with a barely audible rumble, letting in a blast of cold early morning air and gusts of rain.

I went back quickly over the apron, keeping the mainbeam and sidelights off. The girl was straining her eyes all round but the silence continued unbroken. The doors slid shut again behind us and then I'd straightened up on the tarmac. I engaged forward gear and we rolled on through the rain.

I felt better then. The wipers were already working overtime now and I put the mainbeam on and idled slowly down toward the front entrance and the buildings of the Mercador Motel. There were already lights in the windows like the staff were up. I stopped near the reception entrance and pounded over under the canopy, the rain whipping at my face. I put the big metal key with the number tag through the letter-box and saw it bounce on the carpet through the glass door.

I got back behind the driving wheel in three seconds flat. The Holm number hadn't ceased her vigilant watch. She'd got a big piece of perspex with ruled lines and calibration marks now. She'd clamped it over a large section of the map and had been studying it until I came up. Now she put it on the dashboard shelf in front of her, where I couldn't read it. I grinned to myself, slamming the driving door.

I gunned on out. Early as we were, there were already three automobiles gassing up at the pumps. I saw a dark-haired girl in a white slicker darting about under the canopy. She gave a brilliant smile of recognition and waved furiously. I gave a low signal on the horn and then Sylvia Ashton's figure had faded in the rear mirror. I felt a small stab of regret. Jenny Holm was watching my face sardonically.

'Sorry I'm spoiling your outing,' she said.

'You're not,' I told her. 'Because of you I'm having a delightful early holiday trip and a several thousand dollar bonus at the end of it.'

She smiled cheerfully and picked up the map section again.

'Which way?' I said.

'Turn right and then stop a hundred yards down. Please.'

I stared at her hard but I did like she said. We sat in a concrete layby at the roadside watching the tarmac being beaten to a frenzy by dancing shards of rain. The girl was slewed in her seat, watching the road behind us.

'I'll have that cup of coffee now, Mr Faraday, if you don't mind.'

'By all means,' I said.

I got the flask from the cubby in front of me, unscrewed the cap, got the cup from inside and poured her a long, hot measure.

'Sugar's in,' I said. 'You do take it?'

She took the cup from me without ceasing to watch the road.

'Thank you. Of course.'

She drank in small sips, holding the pistol in her disengaged hand. I watched the road in the rear mirror too. At almost the same instant one of the cars at the filling station gunned out. It turned left, down the steep road in the general direction of L.A. I stayed put and said nothing. We sat there for another ten minutes. The other two cars came out. Both of them turned

144

toward L.A. too. The girl leaned toward me with a sigh of relief.

'Just making sure. You may drive on.'

She was beginning to treat me like a chauffeur but I was starting to enjoy it.

'Sure,' I said. 'Just let me know when and where to steer.'

Jenny Holm looked at me sharply.

'I'll do that,' she said drily.

I let in the gear and the big car glided forward. We started making time through the gloom and the cold and the driving rain.

2

We drove for about five hours. We were on secondary roads, mostly, that twisted and turned up into the mountains. She, or Ingolstadt, had chosen lonely country that didn't contain many houses or generate much traffic and any other time and in other weather I would have maybe enjoyed it. But with the rain sheeting down, the tyres slipping on the edges of exposed roads where only a flimsy guard-rail protected the Caddy from five-hundred feet drops into ravines, and the general depressing lack of visibility, it was no fun.

The girl said nothing at first, just keeping on with her map-reading, and now and again giving monosyllabic instructions for turning or retracing our tracks. For we were certainly going round in gigantic circles the higher we climbed and I realized after a while that Ingolstadt had carefully plotted the route. It added to my confusion if anything.

While it was calculated to put any possible pursuers off it also had an entirely opposite purpose; for if Comstock or his mob were monitoring us by radio they had only to stay still and we'd come back toward them in tantalizingly dangerous sweeps. Something of my suspicions must have communicated themselves to Jenny Holm for she said at last.

'Mr Ingolstadt knows what he's doing, Mr Faraday. All we have to do is follow the route laid out. There won't be any danger to either of us until tonight.'

'We'll need some more gas before then,' I said.

The girl shook her head, smiling.

'He thought of that too. There's fifteen gallons stacked away in the boot, inside those cardboard fruit boxes.'

I looked at her closely.

'Fine. Let's hope he's got some more aces up his sleeve. Like some bullet-proof vests for the end of the road.'

She chuckled quietly to herself.

'I wouldn't put it past him, Mr Faraday. This is a first-rate operation. It should succeed.'

It was light by this time and with daylight

and another coffee my mood was changing. Maybe things would turn out all right. I didn't mind a situation where I was calling all the shots and I had calculated the possibilities myself. But Ingolstadt hadn't levelled at all with me so far and I would be crazy to entirely trust the girl, especially after what I'd found out. After all, she was a mobster's woman and she was just as likely to use her pistol on me in an emergency, despite her nice manners.

You're becoming cynical, Mike, I told myself. I spun the wheel to the right like the girl said, and we rocketed upward, through a narrow pass, the blunt hills fringed with heavy green foliage that the rain was dampening nicely. But it was less heavy than it had been and there was even a hint of sun through the clouds.

'North or south this time,' I said.

'North,' the girl said. 'Another fifteen miles before we turn again.'

I nodded, changing gear and putting my foot down a little on the accelerator. We hadn't seen any other traffic at all for the past twenty minutes and I was as certain as could be that nothing was following us. Leastways, for the last five miles. It didn't really matter because anyone reading our signals could stay twenty miles back and still keep track.

'What about lunch?' I said.

'In another fifteen minutes,' she said.

She was looking to the right-hand side of the

road and in a few more minutes I saw what she was searching for. It was nothing more than a single track of loose scree that went straight up like a white blaze in the green of the forest land. It was just wide enough for one car and the terrain shelved steeply either side.

We pulled off the road and bored on up, the Caddy rocking violently like we were at sea. At the top there was a heavy formation of natural rock, about thirty feet high, from which one would get a good view of the surrounding country. The track widened out and went clear around the base of the rocks, re-joining the road in front. I pulled the Caddy in at the rear, where we were hidden from the road.

'It's part of an old fire-break system,' the girl explained, pointing away down the hill behind us, where the trees had been chopped back and the remains of the gravel surface overgrown by grass and weeds. I got out the car and stretched my legs. The rain had stopped now and I could hear the hum of a car coming up the highway below. I got to the edge of the rocks and looked around. It passed on into the distance without decreasing speed.

I eased back in the car and looked at the fuel-gauge. The tank was almost half-empty already.

'I'll gas up after we eat,' I told the girl. 'As good a place as any.'

'Fine. Now the rain's stopped we'll picnic on top of the rocks. That way we can watch the

148

road too.'

I got the flask, the sandwiches and some fruit Sylvia Ashton had put up. By the time I joined her Jenny Holm had already found a sheltered spot, just below the crest of the limestone, and had spread her raincoat for a place to sit. We ate our lunch in silence, looking at the dark thread of road below as though a threat would manifest itself along its innocent length at any moment.

CHAPTER SEVENTEEN

1

It was raining again. I stared through the starred windshield, turning the wheel automatically at the girl's laconically whispered instructions. There was nothing in all the sodden ribbon of black highway either coming toward us or behind, which at least made for more relaxed driving, but we'd turned and back-tracked so many times in the last two hours that I was becoming as confused in my directions as my thoughts.

I shot a sidelong glance at the girl but her tense, concentrated face told me nothing. She wore the dark scarf arrangement which concealed the soft outline of her left cheek and she had her pistol down on the seat at her side. Right now she had the thick perspex sheet with its grid-markings clamped down over the new section of large-scale map and was studying it with concentration.

'Great,' she said at last. 'An ideal location.'

'I wish you'd tell me,' I said. 'I'll be unfit for normal driving by the time this case is over.'

She smiled, revealing the perfect teeth.

'Stop exaggerating, Mr Faraday. Apart from your minor frustrations regarding our destination, this operation has gone like clockwork so far.'

'Too much like clockwork,' I said. 'Clockwork falls apart sometimes.'

I glanced at the sodden landscape around us with distaste.

'Supposing Comstock's mob is coming toward us, for example.'

She shot me a quick glance.

'What do you mean?'

'What I say,' I said. 'They may be zeroing in on us from the north. From the San Francisco direction.'

I realized I'd made a mistake but it was too late to back out now.

'What are you driving at, Mr Faraday?'

'They might just know where we're going,' I said. 'Have you ever thought of that? Maybe they don't need to follow us. Maybe they know our destination already.'

The girl shook her head vehemently.

'Quite impossible, Mr Faraday.'

'I don't see how you can say that, Miss Holm,' I told her. 'There may have been a leak somewhere. In Mr Ingolstadt's office, for example.'

Jenny Holm stared at me in a moody silence.

'You're a pretty smart man, Mr Faraday, but I think you're on the wrong tack,' she said at last.

I shrugged.

'Have it your way. Let's hope you're right. You want another sandwich? We got some more here.'

She waved away the proffered package.

'I have other things to think about. We should be dead on schedule.'

'I hope so,' I said. 'It will be dark inside two hours.'

I looked across at the map.

'You got the co-ordinates all right?'

She nodded.

'I have them, Mr Faraday. Though I hope we won't have any difficulty finding our destination.'

I concentrated on the road again. A truck was coming down toward us, its headlights undipped. The dazzle made a glare on the screen and he only dipped them when I flipped my mainbeams on.

'What makes you say that?'

Jenny Holm frowned.

'There doesn't seem to be anything there,

that's all. The map gives only lake and forest.'

I looked at her thoughtfully.

'There must be something. If you want my opinion I think we ought to go straight there and not wait for dark.'

The girl looked at me gloomily. For the first time there was doubt on her face.

'You may be right, Mr Faraday. But Mr Ingolstadt was adamant that we should arrive around dusk. Timing was important, he said.'

We were going uphill again now, the sky still dark and louring, the dark mass of trees and evergreens coming down the hillsides in heavy sweeps toward the road. There was nothing behind us at all and the dampness and cheerlessness of the surroundings seemed to come right into the car with a palpable presence.

The girl was silent for a moment or two longer, drumming nervously with her fingers on the heavy plastic bearing the co-ordinates. She still wore the black outfit she had on when I met her off the plane but I'd gotten used to it by now.

'Let's compromise, Mr Faraday. Let's circle around for another half-hour, then make straight for our destination. We'll arrive half an hour before dusk and that will give us time to get our bearings.'

'Suits me,' I said. 'I'm tired of all this fooling.'

I glanced at the fuel gauge. We still had half a

tank and there was plenty of gasoline left in the boot.

'Turn again here, Mr Faraday.'

I did like she said, the Caddy's tyres rumbling on the rough surface of the secondary road, the water drumming sombrely on the roof and sluicing up from beneath the wheels. We were going uphill but now the terrain was beginning to level out. It was still pretty savage and we drove on until the girl gave me an order to turn to the left again.

'We're going straight there,' she said quietly. 'I want to get this over as much as you do.'

'Worried about the meeting with Sternwood?' I said.

She compressed her lips tightly.

'It won't be easy.'

'How long since you've seen him?'

She lit a cigarette with jerky, nervous movements, putting the matchstalk in the dashboard tray.

'Almost a year now.'

I spun the wheel again as we came to a fork, following the girl's pointing finger. We were in a deep tunnel of boughs as the road ran straight through an avenue of chestnut trees. The rain was increasing if anything.

'There should be a small village up ahead, Mr Faraday. It's called Crestville. The place we want is about fifteen miles north of that.'

'All right,' I said. 'I'll find it.'

I put my foot down on the accelerator and

153

we started making time.

2

It was getting quite dark when we got up there but I guessed that was because the clouds were so heavy and low. Normally, there would have been almost another hour of daylight. I stopped the Caddy on the narrow lane while the girl consulted the map again. There was the steely glint of water through the trees.

She passed the map to me in the end.

'That's it, Mr Faraday. You can see why I was confused.'

I studied the co-ordinates carefully. HG5824 and LX3109 crossed exactly in the middle of what appeared to be forest land. The only nearby feature was a lake. I looked up from the map at the distant glimmer of water. Maybe this one?

'Seems screwy,' I said, handing the map back. 'But perhaps there's something up there. Some sort of memorial?'

'We'll see, Mr Faraday,' she said in a worried voice. 'I just wanted to get your opinion.'

'How come Ingolstadt didn't tell you exactly where you were going?' I said.

Jenny Holm shook her head.

'He's a cagey old bird. He said this business had to be played his way or not at all.'

'So there were some things he didn't even tell you?'

'That's right.'

I spun the wheel again, taking a fork which led in the general direction of the lake. We were going steeply uphill and I changed down, the car settling more comfortably to the long haul, the lane twisting and turning so that we seemed to be coming back on our own tracks. But we'd been doing that for hours anyway, so it seemed pretty normal to me.

'Keep an eye on those co-ordinates,' I said. 'Is this road marked?'

'I've got it but we appear to be a little off course. We're going to the right.'

'It can't be far off,' I said, as a big sheet of water started coming into view between the bare branches of trees. We were looking down on the lake now and its dark surface was agitated by the wind and churned to whiteness by the fury of the rain.

Almost as soon as I spoke the lane started in a gentle curve to the left and began to descend toward the shore-line; I saw Jenny Holm's face bent in concentration over the map. I kept a sharp eye in the rear-mirror but there was still a blank. If I hadn't known about the bug under the car I would have sworn nobody except a bird could have followed us up here. But I was certain there was nothing within five miles of us.

The last automobile we'd seen was way back

in one of the only two streets that made up Crestville. The girl was silent as she studied the map and I was concentrating on the steering. We were running parallel with the lake now, about thirty or forty feet above water-level, and the road was dark and heavy with the encroaching shadows of the trees. I was steering on sidelights only and I needed all my attention for the road.

Then we were out of the dark tunnel and the girl spoke again.

'We're beginning to close on the co-ordinates.'

'That's something,' I said.

The road was curving away from the lake and we were almost down at its level so that it had disappeared below the trees though I could still see its reflection lightening the sky. The road opened out and we came at last on to the broad foreshore. I began to see what Ingolstadt was at. There couldn't have been a more remote or more secure spot for such a meeting as that between Sternwood and the girl.

She shot me a quick glance as though she had guessed what I was thinking and then bent over the map again. The road was still curved to the left away from this section of lake and followed the woodland around, back from the shore. Jenny Holm looked puzzled.

'We can't be more than half a mile off,' she said.

I tooled the Caddy round several more

hairpins, my thoughts ricochetting around in my mind with more action than a pin-table. Now we were coming to a sort of asphalt clearing in the forest, which led to two big brick entrance gates. Rusty iron hung at a crazy angle and there were weeds growing knee-high. A drive curved away into thick undergrowth and a board wired to one of the gates bore in almost obliterated letters the legend: TO LET.

I braked the car and stopped in the middle of the roundabout. Jenny Holm looked frankly disbelieving.

'This can't be it?'

I nodded.

'It is. The old Greeley estate.'

'You know it, then?'

'Not exactly,' I said. 'But I read about it in newspapers and magazines. It's been empty for over thirty years, ever since old man Greeley died. He was known as the Copper King. He wanted to outdo Citizen Kane and over-reached himself.'

The girl's green eyes were puzzled.

'What do you mean?'

'He built this fantastic mansion,' I said. 'He lost his fortune on it. When he died most of it was demolished to pay his debts. They wanted to let or sell it after all the paintings and valuables had been sold but no-one would take it on. So they tore it down and the estate just went back to forest.'

The girl looked at me, still with the

disbelieving expression; then switched her eyes on to the entrance gates and the dancing shards of rain in the falling light.

'You think this is the rendezvous?'

'Why not,' I said. 'It would be ideal from Sternwood's point of view. Let's give it a whirl.'

I drove the Caddy in through the gates, the bodywork making a crackling noise as it brushed the long grass and undergrowth which completely choked the driveway.

'You'd better check the co-ordinates again,' I said.

I had the mainbeams on now and they stencilled a yellow glare ahead of us. The girl bent to the map, using the swivel light on the dash.

'They converge exactly.'

'No doubt, then,' I said. 'If old man Ingolstadt knows what he's doing we can't go wrong.'

I drove on. The approach to the mansion was a long one but there was plenty of light in the sky as we came out from the trees on to what had once evidently been parkland and formal garden. I could see the trace of a tarmac road and I followed it around, searching for the remains of the house.

The lake was again to our right as the trees thinned away and its burnished surface looked like a steel shield ruffled by the falling rain and the wind. We passed some overgrown tennis

158

courts whose netting was a support for vine and shoots of rhododendron which had grown wild and presently I pulled the Caddy up in front of a great flight of stone steps, barely visible beneath their thick mat of weeds.

'This must be it,' I said.

I got out the car, put my raincoat on swiftly. The girl was already out the other side, belting hers. I saw she had the pistol ready in her hand and I got the Smith-Wesson out and put it in my right-hand pocket, my hand on the butt. We went up the steps two at a time. At the top the house was nothing but a tumbled mass of masonry.

We slowly approached what had once been the front door. There was the remains of a massive Palladian porch, made of granite and evidently destined to stand for all time. There were pools of water on the terrace and what had once been the interior of the mansion was filled with black, stagnant slime which reflected back the fading daylight like a steel engraving.

'In Xanadu did Kubla Khan ...' I said.

The girl looked at me, smiling gravely.

'You can say that again, Mr Faraday.'

Somehow I was certain then she wasn't what she seemed. I looked round quickly in the growing dusk. There was nobody around, that was for sure. A helicopter passed in the far distance, dipping across the lake, its navigation lights winking. It passed on toward the south, the beat of its motor growing fainter until it was lost.

'What exactly did Ingolstadt say?' I asked.

'He said the summer-house,' the girl went on. 'But there isn't a summer-house.'

'That's where you're wrong,' I said. 'You should have been less tight-mouthed. It was in this magazine supplement I read. It's a sort of Greek temple, on an island out in the lake.'

I pointed across the water. Something white glimmered in the dark mass of land about a mile off-shore. The girl was already running down the steps and I sprinted after her. She was something of an athlete because I had a job to catch her. It took us only a few minutes to reach the shore.

The filigree-work of a rusted pier stood out in silhouette a short distance along. Several boats bobbed at anchor; there were half a dozen row-boats and a couple of cabin cruisers. I stopped, looking round in the failing light.

'Odd isn't it?' I said. 'All this stuff for a deserted estate and a deserted island.'

'For God's sake, Mr Faraday!' the girl said impatiently. 'This is no time to think things out. Do that on the way over.'

She had a point so I threw off the two mooring ropes and jumped aboard. The girl was already pushing us off the pier with her foot. We drifted while I fiddled with the outboard. To my surprise it was a fairly new Seagull and it fired the third time I pulled the toggle. I looked at her in suspicion.

'Curiouser and curiouser.'

The girl went to stand by the cabin entrance. I'd already looked in there. There was no-one aboard the craft except us. She had regained something of her old manner now.

'Mr Sternwood will explain. Let's just get across.'

I steered up wind of the island, hardly conscious of the driving rain and the wind out here which was making the water choppy. The outlines were growing thicker and more distinct. We were already halfway across. The girl stood looking stonily ahead, as if all her future lay in the white outlines of the building which was slowly composing itself out of the fading light.

I put the Smith-Wesson in my shoulder holster, turned my head away out of the wind. Instinctively, I looked back at the shore. The outlines of the pier were sharp and distinct now against the grey water.

There were three black silhouettes on the pier. Even as I watched they seemed to flicker and disappear. I didn't tell the girl. There was no point for the moment. I steered the boat and watched the white building grow in clarity and definition with every second that passed.

CHAPTER EIGHTEEN

1

Jenny Holm had jumped ashore before I could tie the boat up at the rough wooden jetty which jutted out from the sandy spit at the tip of the island. She waited for me, the pistol held down by the side of her handbag, as she looked about her. I killed the motor and took a turn around a big wooden pile with the stern-rope.

'Hold that,' I told the girl.

She made an expert job of tying up while I went forward and uncoiled the mooring rope. By the time I'd jumped ashore and made fast the dusk was thick, making clotted, indistinct shapes of the foliage along the shore-line.

'The temple's over there,' I said, pointing to the left.

Jenny Holm nodded, her face huddled into the collar of her white raincoat, the rain beating unheeded against her face. I stepped out beside her, holding the Smith-Wesson ready. I glanced back once or twice across the lake but there was nothing visible against the dark blur of the far shore that marked the Greeley estate.

We walked in silence, following a beaten path through the bushes. There were no other boats tied at the pier or drawn up on the shore, not even a row-boat, and I wondered how Sternwood would have gotten to the island. Perhaps the figures I'd seen on the pier were his men, making sure we kept our part of the bargain; and they'd already run him across.

Or maybe he'd come from the opposite shore of the lake and his boat was over there waiting to take him and his evidence back. And maybe Jenny Holm too? I hadn't thought of that. I looked at her carefully as we brushed through the wet, heavy foliage, following the indistinct path that led upward from the open shore. I was on her right-hand side now and she was showing a clear profile. She looked pretty sensational without the scarf on this side and she would have been an exceptionally striking woman without the scar. Assuming my hunch was wrong and that she still carried it. Maybe I'd find out before this evening was over.

'What happens now?' I said. 'Assuming Sternwood's there?'

She gave me a sidelong glance.

'He'll be there,' she said confidently.

The path narrowed then and she went ahead of me, holding back the small bough of a tree so that I could brush beneath.

'I don't understand your question.'

'It's not very difficult,' I said.

We were walking alongside each other again now, as the path broadened out, the heavy trees falling back a little in the twilight.

'After you've given Sternwood the evidence. Do you go back with him? Or stay with me?'

She looked at me curiously.

'I thought I'd made my position very clear, Mr Faraday. I'm fulfilling an obligation. Nothing more. Naturally, after we've seen Sternwood and I've talked with him and given him what I came to give him, I'll be going back. With you, I mean.'

I nodded.

'Fair enough. Just so I know what the score is. It's about the only advance piece of information I've been given on this job.'

The girl smiled. She put her hand gently on my arm.

'Poor Mr Faraday. It's been a bore to you, hasn't it?'

'Hardly,' I said. 'But it'll be rich Mr Faraday if this comes out all right.'

She held her head on one side as she studied my face.

'In my terms,' I told her. 'Like I said I operate strictly at the gritty end of the market.'

The trees were dropping back and it was becoming a little lighter now that their heavy shadows were removed. The rain still fell heavily, drumming on the leaves and making furtive rustling noises that made it seem like we were being followed all the time. On three occasions I'd turned in the past five minutes, the Smith-Wesson at the ready, expecting to see someone on the path behind us.

It wasn't good for the nerves and normally mine are pretty steady. I realized why Ingolstadt had chosen the rendezvous here. It was the best from our point of view. Once we were in the summer-house we had a clear field of fire across open ground, right to the edge of the tree-line.

We were picking our way across what had been open parkland and I tightened my collar to keep out the driving rain. The girl was in front again and I pulled her back level. With our light clothing in the dusk we'd be first-rate targets if there was anyone hostile waiting in the summer-house.

Like before Jenny Holm seemed to read my thoughts. She put her right hand through my arm familiarly, still keeping hold of her pistol. We must have looked a pretty funny couple had there been anyone to see.

'Don't worry, Mr Faraday. Sternwood will be there. And there will be no tricks. The danger is behind us.'

'You may be speaking a greater truth than you think,' I said.

I cast a glance back over my shoulder at the blurred, impenetrable mass of the trees behind us. We were on an asphalt path and our feet made loud gritting noises, despite the blanketing of moss and coarse grass. We passed the ruins of a fountain, its basins full of water again, making white rivulets in the growing darkness as they overflowed, one into the other.

The shape of the summer-house was growing before us with every step we took. It was on a mound at the far end of the valley, about three hundred yards off and the scale of the place made it obvious that the lay-out here must have been really something in old man Greeley's time.

There were sets of stone steps with balustrades up from the bottom of the mound to the terrace on which the summer-house sat, and the moss and lichen made a sickly patina against the white of the stone.

I turned as we got to the bottom and raked the valley with my eyes. There was still nothing but the feeling I'd had ever since the case began persisted. It just didn't sit right and there was no telling myself it did. I sighed heavily and followed Jenny Holm who was leading the way up the first flight of steps with a springy stride. I followed on a little more cautiously; it was treacherous underfoot here and the moss was extremely slippery.

Jenny Holm was already halfway across the first terrace before I got up.

'Don't get too far ahead,' I warned. 'I'm responsible for your safety.'

She waited obediently for me until I drew level and we went up the next flight together.

'Sorry, Mr Faraday. I tend to forget these things.'

I nodded.

'We still don't know what we're going to find up top.'

'I know,' she said confidently.

'Maybe,' I told her. 'But you're still my responsibility. And I promised Ingolstadt. So I get to the summer-house first.'

She shrugged.

'As you wish. I suppose I ought to be grateful.'

'You're good at running,' I said. 'If I get the chop you can light out.'

She stared at me gravely, her features indistinct in the gathering darkness.

'That's not funny, Mr Faraday. Please don't suggest such a thing.'

'Sure,' I said. 'I'm not anxious for it to happen but I'm just pointing out the possibilities.'

We were going up the last flight now and the rain seemed to slacken a little. Not that it mattered. We couldn't get any wetter than we already were. I went ahead of the girl, stopped on the last terrace. The place was bigger than I thought. There were two big stone shelters near where I was standing on the terrace. They had stone ornamental seats inside them. Up a more shallow flight about ten yards farther back stood the summer-house itself.

It was circular in shape, apparently of white marble, with graceful pillars curving up toward the domed roof. The pillars continued round until they were lost in the gloom. The front made a big open porch that was completely black, which told me two things. It had no door and the interior was filled in, otherwise the light from the sky would have shone straight through.

It was the perfect place for an ambush. Anyone standing on the steps would have stood no chance against someone firing from inside the interior of the dome. A nerve in my cheek twitched as I stood there. I saw the girl move out the corner of my eye as she came up a couple of steps.

'Stay where you are,' I said.

I went on up the last flight, between the two small porchlike structures, my size nines slapping back echoes from the wet marble, the rain stinging my face and eyes. As cases went this was about the apex of my career. Whatever that meant. About two feet from the bottom of the pile probably. I got on to the final terrace and stayed there.

I stood for perhaps ten seconds. I'd never felt more exposed in my life. A figure was slowly coming out the doorway. A tall man with a white belted raincoat like my own. He stood there like he was the brooding spirit of the place. He had his hands deep in his pockets.

'Mr Sternwood, I presume?' I said.

'You are correct, Mr Faraday,' he said ironically. 'You have Miss Holm with you, I take it?'

'She's here all right,' I said.

168

'Then kindly send her in.'

Before I could move Jenny Holm had clattered past me on her high heels. She went on walking confidently up the terrace toward the waiting figure. I stood with my hand on the butt of the Smith-Wesson and waited for something to happen.

2

Nothing did. The girl got up to Sternwood and they stood deep in conversation for a couple of minutes. There seemed nothing affectionate or informal about the meeting. I don't know what I'd expected. I glanced back down the steps once or twice but there was nothing but the empty valley and the sheeting rain. The two went on talking quietly under the entrance to the big dome. Then the girl turned, her hand on the tall man's arm. But it was Sternwood who spoke.

'Please come in, Mr Faraday. You've done a good job. There's nothing to fear from me, I can assure you.'

'It's just my natural caution,' I said.

I kept my hand on the butt of the Smith-Wesson and walked up toward them. The rain ceased as I got up close and I realized the marble flooring was dry. I looked up. The big dome of the porch extended some ten feet forward at this point. The tall man turned, like he wanted to keep his face hidden.

'Let us go inside,' he said. 'This will take a few minutes.'

The girl shot me a warning glance, but the tall man was walking ahead as if this were the most normal meeting in the world.

'How did you get here?' I asked his impassive back.

'That is restricted information, Mr Faraday. You will be told in good time.'

Another puzzle. His voice was cultured, well-educated. If this was the head of a hoodlum empire it was a university-educated one. For the first time I understood Sternwood's appeal for a girl like Jenny Holm. They must have been two like minds; on the side of crime.

It was lighter in the dome than I figured. My eyes were getting used to it now. There was a wooden floor here, on which our feet echoed and there seemed to be more than one room.

There were several windows, still with glass in, on each side, and they cast a feeble radiance over the floor so that we seemed to be standing in one of those eighteenth-century paintings, in which the only illumination comes from the dying light of dusk. I always found them pretty gloomy myself but there was no accounting for taste.

There were some rustic wooden chairs and tables scattered about and Sternwood seated himself near one of the dusty windows, facing

170

the open entrance to the dome, overlooking the steps up which we'd come. A red light suddenly glowed in the darkness. I had the gun up in my pocket but Jenny Holm put her hand on my arm, forcing the muzzle down.

Sternwood had picked up the black plastic mouthpiece now.

'Everything in order,' he said. 'Mr Faraday and the girl have arrived.'

He listened intently as a low, garbled voice sounded in the headset for a minute or so. He looked approvingly at the girl and me.

'Excellent,' he said softly. 'In about a quarter of an hour then.'

He put the mouthpiece down on the table and glanced at me almost abstractedly.

'You seem well organized, Mr Sternwood.'

'I am always well organized.'

His ice-blue eyes turned from me to the girl.

'You haven't changed, Jenny.'

'Neither have you.'

He was silent for a moment, drumming with thin, sensitive fingers on the pitted surface of the table. He wasn't at all what I'd expected. He was about forty or forty-five years old, with a lean body and tanned features. He had short blond hair which had no touch of grey; it was expensively barbered and now glistening with drops of rain. His eyes were expressive and mobile underneath the thin blond eyebrows.

His nose was straight; the mouth firm and intelligent; the cheekbones high; the jaw square

171

and strong. His teeth, when he spoke, were white and even. Altogether he looked like a minor film-star; one of those fairly good-looking men who never made top billings on the marquees but were usually second leads; the close friends of Ronald Colman or David Niven. Philip Friend or Patric Knowles would have been about the mark.

The raincoat must have cost a lot of money; under it I could glimpse an impeccably cut pale grey lightweight suit worn over a cream silk shirt and a pale blue wool tie. He seemed unaware of my scrutiny though I could see a smile beginning at the corners of his mouth. But he ignored me, turned to the girl.

'You brought the stuff, of course?'

'Of course,' she said.

She rummaged in her handbag, came up with a flat package in brown paper, very like the one Ingolstadt had fobbed me off with. She smiled suddenly like the same thought had crossed her mind.

'No, Mr Faraday. It's the real thing this time.'

'I should hope so,' I said. 'Mr Sternwood may not be so amiable as me.'

The lean man in the white raincoat flashed a brief smile. He reached over for the package the girl held out. I stood up suddenly. Sternwood crouched like a panther on the wooden bench, his eyes very wide and alert.

'What's the matter, Mr Faraday?'

172

'We may have been followed,' I said. 'I don't aim to get jumped.'

He shrugged.

'Do your job then. Don't mind us.'

I turned away as he started tearing the paper off the package. I crossed the floor in quick strides, got behind one of the big entrance pillars. There was nothing moving in the whole of the valley except the tops of the trees and the falling rain. I left the Smith-Wesson in my raincoat pocket and prowled round the room, looking through the windows. I couldn't see anything there either. The back of the dome was solid stone and there was no way in.

There was a small flight of steps here that led up to a wooden door. I had my foot on the steps when Sternwood addressed me in a curt voice.

'There's nothing up there that concerns you, Mr Faraday.'

I came back down.

'As you wish. You're calling the shots.'

'So long as you remember it.'

I stared at him for a moment. He was using my dialogue. But I didn't tell him that.

'There's something I don't understand, Mr Sternwood,' I said.

He smiled thinly, his watchful eyes never leaving my face. He had the big black notebook on the table and now he re-wrapped it without looking down, jammed it in his raincoat pocket.

'There's a lot of things you don't understand, Mr Faraday.'

'That's true,' I said. 'But I'm talking about one point in particular.'

Jenny Holm looked at me warningly. Sternwood sat at ease at the table, motionless except for the slight drumming of his fingers on the wooden top.

'Be my guest.'

'Miss Holm's your witness,' I said. 'The only thing between you and a capital sentence. Yet she's coming back with me. I thought the whole idea was that she should stay with you and work on your defence.'

Jenny Holm bit her lip but Sternwood merely gave her another of his thin smiles.

'An interesting question, Mr Faraday. And one difficult to answer at this point in time.'

There was a sudden explosion from the valley below which tore at my nerves and something went whining off one of the entrance pillars to the summer-house, sending chips of marble dancing about the interior. The girl was on one knee already, the pistol in her hand. Sternwood gave me a twisted smile. A blued-steel automatic had grown in his fist.

'Fortunately, Mr Faraday, your question is likely to be academic now,' he said lightly.

He gestured toward the doorway.

'I think it is time to earn your keep.'

I took the Smith-Wesson out my pocket, threw off the safety. I got out on the porch,

174

keeping one of the big pillars between me and the flight of steps. I looked downward through the dusk and the falling rain.

Three men were standing on the first terrace at the bottom of the staircase. Two of them were holding sub-machine guns in their hands and they looked like they could use them.

CHAPTER NINETEEN

1

'It's getting rather crowded round here,' I said.

The taller of the three made an impatient gesture with his shoulders. He was dressed in a dark stormproof coat and he was the only one who didn't seem to be carrying a gun.

'It's Mr Faraday, isn't it?'

'As if you didn't know,' I said. 'You're Mr Comstock, I take it?'

The tall man made another impatient gesture.

'Never mind who I am, Faraday. I want Jenny Holm and I mean to have her. We can do this the easy way or a lot of people get killed. It makes no matter to me. But it just might to you.'

'You have a point,' I said.

'We can't stand here getting soaked,' the tall

man said in a flat voice. 'We're coming up.'

'You better not do that,' I said. 'I'll come down. It will be drier in one of those shelters.'

The tall man debated for a moment, like he wasn't used to being given suggestions. Then he made up his mind.

'All right, Mr Faraday. But no tricks.'

'No tricks,' I said.

I left the Smith-Wesson in my pocket and walked slowly down the steps. The two men with the sub-machine guns went into the right-hand shelter. The man in the dark coat remained on the terrace until I joined him. His face was olive-coloured and impassive. He wore a black homburg hat which made him look like a New York stockjobber. He had the narrowest and deadliest eyes I'd ever seen.

Comstock looked at me with as little emotion as if I'd been a fly on the back of his hand.

'Before we talk, Mr Faraday,' he said in the same flat voice. 'I may as well tell you we have another seven men back in the trees there. That makes ten against three, if you can count.'

'I can count,' I said.

The cogs of my mind were racing round uselessly now. I couldn't think of anything. While the cogs were still racing Comstock turned his back to me and walked into the left-hand, empty shelter. I followed him in. There didn't seem to be much else to do. He turned to face me, his eyes boring into mine. In the dim light his face looked like bronze.

'Those men can be here in a few seconds at the first shot. So be very careful.'

'Oh, I'll be that all right,' I said.

'Good,' he said.

He sat down carefully on one of the stone benches in the shelter, crossing his legs. He was so confident of himself and his power that the men with the sub-machine guns weren't even in sight. I heard the scrape of a match from the other shelter as one of them lit a cigarette.

'You've been engaged to guard Miss Holm on her journey I understand.'

It was a statement of fact, not a question, but I wasn't inclined to help him.

'You could call it that,' I said.

The bronze face swivelled to look at me. The man's body was completely immobile. I decided not to fool around with him. He was one of those characters entirely without nerves; a man who would strike as quickly as a snake and just as lethal.

'Come, Mr Faraday, don't let's play games. We've had you under observation ever since you left L.A. International.'

'I knew all about the bug under the car.' I said.

The eyes flickered momentarily; they were almost black and as they turned from me to gaze out at the sodden landscape of the Greeley estate, which was slowly being effaced by the dusk, there was an almost palpable menace in them.

'In that case why didn't you remove it?'

'I always like to see my cases out,' I said.

He moved slightly, his face heavy with thought.

'An admirable precept, Mr Faraday. But one you will find a matter of regret unless you do as I say.'

I reached in my left-hand breast-pocket for my package of cigarettes; something moved in the dusk and one of the big men from the flanking shelter was standing there. The muzzle of the sub-machine gun was aligned rock-steady on my gut.

'I'd like to smoke,' I said.

Comstock nodded.

'You have a pistol in your right-hand raincoat pocket. I would advise you not to attempt to use it.'

'I don't aim to commit suicide,' I said.

I got my cigarettes and lit up, feathering smoke through my nostrils.

'Excellent,' the man with the bronze face went on.

I glanced out the shelter again. The big man was still standing there, oblivious of the rain.

'But we were talking about what you must do.'

I turned back to face him.

'That is?'

'I want to see Jenny Holm.'

'She may not want to see you,' I said.

He shook his head impatiently, his eyes flickering.

'That is irrelevant. We can simply kill you now and go up. Or we can go up together in a friendly manner.'

I nodded.

'It seems I have little choice.'

The man in the dark coat shrugged, his bronze face directed beyond me at the sheets of falling rain.

'You are a realist, Mr Faraday. I admire that quality in a man.'

He stood up, his feet scraping on the stone floor. I flipped my half-smoked cigarette away. It described a fiery arc through the air, before sputtering on the steps in a shower of tiny sparks. It winked out then. Like myself and Jenny Holm and Sternwood if I didn't come up with something soon. The two big men were standing near us now, impassive in the rain and the dusk. Comstock led the way toward the steps, the two men with the automatic weapons following.

'Just a minute,' I said.

The tall man paused, his foot on the first step of the flight.

'Fair's fair,' I said. 'There are only three of us, including the girl. Get one of your men to wait down here. One chopper's enough.'

The bronze face slightly distorted. I guess the expression was meant to indicate a smile.

'As you wish, Mr Faraday. Just so long as

you remember my companion can cut you in half within a second. And naturally, I am armed myself.'

'Naturally,' I said.

Comstock made a tiny, almost invisible gesture and the smaller of the two men melted back down the steps. He stood in the lee of the shelter, looking up toward us.

'Remember, Mr Faraday, we can summon up reinforcements very quickly.'

'I'll remember,' I said.

The big man with the sub-machine gun was on my left; it would make it very awkward if I wanted to drop him with the Smith-Wesson. Almost impossible, in fact. Comstock walked next to me and I had no doubt his hand was on the butt of his own gun in his raincoat pocket. I didn't yet know whether he was right or left-handed. That could be vital if something went wrong.

It would certainly go wrong. Comstock and his boys weren't present in such strength because they were rain-worshippers. They intended to chop Sternwood and the girl. I had no brief for either of them but I'd taken the commission and I'd promised Ingolstadt. As things stood it would be a miracle if I came out on my feet. I almost certainly wouldn't because Comstock would never leave me around to testify against him.

Looks like a nice one, Mike, I told myself. The rain was cold and stinging on my face as we walked on up the steps and toward the black entrance of the summer-house.

2

Comstock stopped when we were about five yards from the massive pillared porch.

'If anything goes wrong you get it first,' he said quietly.

I didn't need the slight swivel of the sub-machine gun barrel at my elbow to get the point.

I stared at the black rectangle in front of us, perspiration beginning to mingle with the rain trickling down my collar. I was already regretting my precipitate action in going down the steps. I should have stayed a few moments and worked out some sort of strategy with Sternwood. It was too late to think of that now.

'You'd better walk in front, Mr Faraday,' the man with the bronze face said quietly.

'The filling in the sandwich,' I said. 'Either way I get it. Back and front.'

'Aptly put. But then you are a professional, are you not? And this is all part of your contract.'

I started forward again, the trigger-man still on my left, but slightly in rear now that we were on the terrace. Comstock was behind me and I could hear his expensive shoes gritting on the wet marble surface. I wondered why neither of them had bothered about my gun. It either displayed complete recklessness or absolute confidence.

Then I remembered there were ten of them. That was an army for this lonely island. And they would know we were only three. They must have watched Sternwood come to the island, through binoculars probably. Though there was a flaw there somewhere. Someone must have brought Sternwood out, unless he'd piloted the boat himself.

I retraced my thoughts. We were only a few feet from the doorway now and it kept my mind off the idea of us silhouetted against the faint light. Comstock and his men had followed us by means of the bugged Caddy; there was nothing unusual about that. But they'd had no means of knowing we were coming to the Greeley estate. Unless they'd got to the lake and Sternwood had gone out to the island round about the same time we'd started; probably from the opposite shore.

The more I thought about it the more likely it seemed. I remembered Sternwood's walkie-talkie and I'd guessed he'd started out as soon as we'd been spotted. Comstock's people could have seen the two boats from the high vantage point of the road which looped round the lake and which we'd taken earlier in the day. There were still a lot of missing factors though.

I hoped Ingolstadt had something up his sleeve. If he hadn't we were all cooked.

Comstock's low voice broke into my whirling thoughts. We were under the dome and the rain was cut off as we faced the dark cave of the interior, only a few feet away.

'Stop here, Mr Faraday. This will do nicely.'

All I could hear now was the heavy beating of my heart, way above even the sullen patter of the rain.

'Jenny!'

Comstock's voice echoed round the interior of the dome.

'We've got your boy-friend. All I want to do is talk. Otherwise, he gets it first and you after.'

There was a long and heavy silence. All I could hear was my heart; even the rain had been erased from my consciousness. I looked back over my shoulder. The man with the bronze face seemed supremely at ease. The last light from the sky turned his face to a texture that resembled beaten gold.

'I am a patient man, Jenny, but I will cut Faraday to pieces if you don't show yourself within thirty seconds. We're coming in anyway. I want your word.'

The girl's voice came then, crisp and confident from the dark interior of the dome.

'All right. So you found us. There's no need for anyone to get hurt.'

Comstock made a strange sound down in his throat that might have passed for a chuckle in a normal person.

'Now you're being sensible. Have we your
183

word?'

'You have my word.'

I looked at Comstock, who moved closer in behind me.

'You're very trusting.'

He shook his head.

'I've never trusted anybody. All we need is a few seconds to get in out the light. I can take care of you and you make a good shield.'

'The people in the dome may be armed,' I said.

'You know they are, Mr Faraday,' he said deliberately. 'They would have been extremely foolish to come here without weapons. But one or two bursts from my colleague here will take care of anyone in the dome. The ricochets would be enough to cut them to pieces. This place is solid stone.'

'You think of everything,' I said.

'No, Mr Faraday. But I try to. Now move.'

I did like he said. There was even less percentage in not doing so. We were spread a little more now. The big man with the sub-machine gun stepped a couple of paces off, turning our party into two groups. Comstock took me by the arm and walked in rear of me. I could feel the muzzle of his pistol against my spine.

'We're coming in, Jenny. Nothing must go wrong.'

The girl's voice came again, confident and clear.

'Nothing can go wrong, providing you play ball. I'll come alone to the middle of the room. We can talk there.'

'Very well.'

The muzzle pressure in my back increased as we passed into the interior of the big central room beneath the dome. The boards beneath our feet echoed and re-echoed. It was dark in here but not so dark as I had imagined. There came again the aroma I'd first noticed when I'd entered the place. It was a mixture of damp, dust and old stone that had a distinctive flavour. It wasn't a particularly happy simile. It was more reminiscent of ancient tombs than anything else. I remembered Jenny Holm's black outfit. I hoped we wouldn't be needing it tonight.

'This will do,' Comstock said.

We stopped up near the rustic table where we'd been before. The big man to my left cleared his throat. I could see more plainly now, the interior of the summer-house slowly coming into focus. The girl stood in back of the table, her hand near the open mouth of her handbag. There was no sign of Sternwood. My eyes instinctively flickered up to the small door at the top of the steps. Comstock had already interpreted the movement.

'Keep your eye on the steps,' he told the trigger-man. 'If anything comes out that door stitch him.'

His eyes were sharper than mine. He'd noted

185

the deeper line of shadow which showed the door was slightly open. I realized something that the bronze-faced man had evidently failed to grasp. However dark it was inside the dome we were still all three silhouetted against the faint light coming in from outside.

Comstock was keeping his intent gaze upon the girl, who stood with head turned down, the scarf still cloaking her features.

'It's been a long time,' he said.

'Long enough,' the girl said.

He made a grimace that seemed like a shudder on his bronze features.

'Absence evidently doesn't make the heart grow fonder,' he said.

The girl gave an impatient shrug.

'After this?'

She pointed savagely at her cheek, still keeping her face toward the table like she was afraid to face the tall man on my right. I was puzzled at her attitude. Seemed like she'd lost her nerve entirely. I glanced round the shadowy dome. If I was relying on Ingolstadt it seemed like I'd missed my guess.

Comstock seemed puzzled too. He was straining his eyes intently through the gloom and he took a brief step toward her. He was now slightly in front of me and my hand closed over the butt of the Smith-Wesson. The sub-machine gun muzzle on my left fanned over, covering me and Comstock. That left the girl out of the line of fire. Comstock seemed to be oblivious of my presence or the trigger-man's now.

'What's the matter with your voice, Jenny?' he said sharply. 'It sounds different, somehow.'

The girl shook her head impatiently.

'It's the dome. Everything echoes in here.'

Comstock took a step back this time, his voice rising slightly, his eyes flickering about.

'It's more than that. What is this?'

The girl raised her head, a smile of triumph on her face. Her fingers were inside the handbag. The faint light from the window struck full on the right-hand side of her face now. Comstock was caught off balance, his face a mask of surprise.

'Why, you're not . . .' he began when the girl got to the pistol and fired through the bottom of the bag. I threw myself to the floor as the machine-gun started blamming.

CHAPTER TWENTY

1

The sound was deafening. The interior of the dome was full of smoke and flying splinters of stone now. I rolled over in the dark, took a chair with me, my finger-tips scrabbling at the butt of the Smith-Wesson as I tried to get it out of my raincoat pocket. Sternwood was suddenly up from the dark below the table edge, the pistol in his hand firing rapidly.

The big man on my left sagged, the muzzle of the sub-machine gun raking the floor. Wood splinters rained around and the table punched away somewhere into the darkness with a tremendous sound like the slamming of a door. Flame and smoke was erupting from Jenny Holm's handbag. Comstock's pistol was still coming clear from his raincoat pocket when the first slug hit him.

It jerked him round so that he was facing me. The light spilling in the open entrance of the dome illuminated his bronze face. He looked like he was doing some deep thinking. While he was deciding about dying Jenny Holm put three more slugs into him.

He went into a crazy dance, suddenly found he was dead. His feet stumbled over my outstretched body and he went face down, black blood descending from his mouth. His homburg rolled across the floor.

Jenny Holm was wiped backward, scarlet spreading on her white raincoat. I started getting to my feet as Sternwood put two more slugs in to the trigger-man. He fired a final burst into the floor and then went over, the sub-machine gun clattering on the boards. A great silence filled the dome and the stink of cordite-smoke was heavy in my nostrils. I put the Smith-Wesson back in my pocket. I hadn't fired a shot in all that time.

I turned as heavy footsteps sounded on the steps outside. The beat of a helicopter surged into the summer-house; it was so low the noise of the rotor-blades was like a savage assault on the eardrums. I remembered then the machine I'd seen over the lake earlier in the day. There was a heavy burst of firing from outside, down the steps, which went on for some time. I got low, keeping well clear of the doorway.

Sternwood was up now, his finger stabbing at something below the table edge. The wail of an automatic klaxon filled the whole of the dome. It was answered from the far distance and muffled gunfire sounded. It came from the woods down near the shore of the island.

I crawled over to the trigger-man, kicked the machine-gun away; the whole of the front of his raincoat was a mass of torn scarlet. I left him then and went out on the terrace. The lights of the helicopter were darting about in mid-air down in the valley. Little sparks were lancing from it. Another klaxon was sounding from the woods and I could see dark figures running.

The second trigger-man was lying halfway down the steps, where he'd fallen. I went down to retrieve his weapon and carried it back into the dome. Sternwood was speaking into a telephone, an intent expression on his face.

'I hope you're satisfied,' I said.

189

His eyes avoided mine. I went over to Jenny Holm. She was lying near the splintered wreckage of the table at the back of the dome. The red was spreading on her white raincoat but her eyes were still open.

I moved her into a more comfortable position. As I was doing it the scarf slipped from her face, revealing a left cheek as smooth and unscarred as the right. While I was thinking about that the blonde wig fell away to the floor.

Long black hair cascaded down her face, completely transforming it. She gave me a crooked grin.

'You're not Jenny Holm,' I said.

'You're an easy man to deceive, Mr Faraday,' she said softly.

I had my handkerchief against her shoulder now. I could see the tear through the back of her coat, where the slug had gone out. It was high up and clear of the bone.

'You're lucky,' I said. 'You're going to be all right.'

I made her comfortable, listening to the distant sound of the klaxon, the racket of the helicopter coming back and the faint noises of firing.

'You certainly meant to get Comstock,' I said. 'It was licensed murder.'

The girl's face clouded with pain as I increased the pressure in staunching the wound.

190

'You don't understand, Mr Faraday.'

'There's a lot of things I don't understand on this case,' I said.

It was quite dark now and beams of lights were dancing up the steps outside. Big men in military-looking uniforms worn under dark slickers pounded into the dome. They carried torches which cast yellow light on the floor and ceiling. The biggest of them saluted Sternwood, who was still on the phone.

'Everything's in hand, sir,' he reported.

The girl smiled at my expression, despite the pain on her features.

A little man with grey hair and an officious manner crossed the floor toward me.

'I'm a doctor,' he said. 'I'll handle this.'

'Be my guest,' I said.

I got up and put the Smith-Wesson away in my shoulder-holster, not knowing the score or hardly what day it was. Reaction was beginning to set in. The dome seemed to be full of people and noise. There was a sudden creaking as the small door at the top of the staircase opened. I stared incredulously. Ingolstadt was coming down the steps, a broad smile on his face. Shelley Beeching was behind him, looking like a fashion plate.

Ingolstadt pumped me by the hand.

'Excellent, Mr Faraday!' he beamed. 'Everything went like clockwork!'

191

'Some clockwork,' I said.

I looked round at the physical and human wreckage on the floor. It was a Shakespearean finale. I got out my pack and reached for a cigarette. I couldn't trust myself to say anything else. Almost before I'd got the smoke to my mouth Ingolstadt lit it for me with a gold lighter.

'We will break the rules for once, Mr Faraday,' he said soothingly. 'You have been under great stress.'

'You can say that again,' I said.

Some of the troopers had hoisted the table and set it upright. It leaned at an angle but it was solid enough. I sank down into a chair behind it and inhaled smoke. The air was tinny with the sound of walkie-talkies and dialogue. The whole dome seemed to be filled with State troopers. Shelley Beeching had a tight, scared expression on her face above the white raincoat, but she had plenty of guts all right.

One of the helicopter crew had produced a sort of plastic hamper. He handed out pre-packed sandwiches, flasks of coffee and bottles of liquor. I suddenly felt ravenously hungry.

'You'd better take a shot of this, Mr Faraday,' Ingolstadt said. 'You're going to be extremely angry and it's bad to be angry on an empty stomach.'

He leaned over and poured some brandy

into my plastic beaker of coffee. I drank it like it had been water. I didn't understand what he was talking about so I didn't react for the moment.

'You two were pretty damn brave holing up in there,' I said, indicating the small room at the top of the staircase. 'How come no-one knew you were here?'

Ingolstadt sat down the other side of the table from me, his wind-swept eyebrows and hair looking as incongruous as ever. He smiled across at Shelley Beeching who sat down next me. One of the troopers carried coffee and spirits over to where the doctor was at work in the corner.

'I would never ask anyone to take risks I was not prepared to take myself,' he said softly. 'Shelley and I came out here this morning to reconnoitre, long before anybody else showed. We were dropped in by helicopter. It was the only way to be sure.'

'Sure of what?' I said.

'Sure of the plan,' Ingolstadt said.

His eyes gleamed as he glanced round the dome.

'One of the biggest clean-up operations ever seen in L.A. And one of which you were a vital part, Mr Faraday. Even if unconsciously.'

The grey-haired doctor was back at Ingolstadt's elbow. He was supporting a white-faced Jenny Holm. He helped her into a seat and Shelley Beeching poured a neat tot of

193

cognac for her.

'She'll do,' the doctor said. 'But we ought to get her back to hospital as soon as possible.'

Ingolstadt nodded.

'The ambulance helicopter will be here shortly.'

He turned to me.

'I'd like you to meet a very brave woman, Mr Faraday. Detective Lieutenant Lauren Jefferies of the New York Police Department.'

My jaw must have hit the top of the table because the girl laughed at my expression. Sternwood had finished telephoning now and sat down at the table opposite. He poured himself a cup of coffee and drank it absently.

'No good my asking who this is?' I said.

Ingolstadt beamed innocently.

'Certainly, Mr Faraday. This is Axel Madsen, L.A.'s new District Attorney. We both owe you a great deal.'

Madsen grinned, fixing me with frank eyes.

'A regrettable deception, Mr Faraday.'

There was a thunderous silence. I was having difficulty in speaking. Shelley Beeching exchanged a conspiratorial glance with the girl I'd known as Jenny Holm. I glanced across at the corpse of the man with the bronze face. The doctor had just turned him over.

'Since I've scored a hundred per cent out of hundred for boners,' I said. 'Would someone mind telling me who that is?'

'By all means, Mr Faraday,' Ingolstadt said

amiably. 'That's what's left of Sternwood.'

3

Ingolstadt's eyes were twinkling with mingled malice and pleasure.

'Just take it in slowly, Mr Faraday, and try not to lose your cool. We deceived you, it is true, but it was vitally necessary if our scheme was to succeed.'

'I haven't got any cool to lose,' I said.

I stared grimly from him to the remains of Sternwood which were now being dragged out the dome by two burly cops wearing storm-capes. Madsen lit a cigarette and feathered out the smoke through his nostrils.

'Just understand our situation, Mr Faraday. I'd been on Sternwood's trail for years, but we could never pin him down on anything. As a practising lawyer I'd amassed a huge dossier on his activities, but I'd never had a chance to bring him to court. The split between Sternwood and Jenny Holm gave us an opportunity to use the girl as a lever.'

He tapped the ash off his cigarette on to the wooden floor, ground it with his heel.

'My appointment as District Attorney a few months ago gave us an ideal opportunity. Sternwood knew of my activities through his manifold contacts, of course. I knew he was out to get me. He could not afford to have me

195

indict him before a Grand Jury. So I knew it was him or me.'

He stared moodily before him at the faint opening in the dome. It was dark outside now but the rotors of the helicopter were still turning and the tinny noises of portable radios went on. I guessed they were getting the worst of the wounded aboard.

'We concocted a scheme, Mr Faraday,' said Ingolstadt slyly. 'A scheme of which you were a vital part. As additional insurance, if you like. Jenny Holm was arrested in New York. On a trumped-up charge, of course.'

He beamed at me as though daring me to interrupt. I was in no mood to do so. I couldn't trust myself to speak.

'We held her incommunicado. It was vital that no word of our plans should leak out. Everyone involved was sworn to secrecy. We gave out that Jenny Holm was to give evidence against Sternwood. We called for volunteers for a dangerous assignment among New York's women police officers. We were given five to choose from. We had to have someone reasonably like Jenny Holm, who was about the same age, fit, and able to use a gun. We chose Lieutenant Jefferies here.'

The girl smiled faintly, holding the beaker of boiling coffee between the fingers of one clenched hand. Her other arm was in a sling and she was supported round the shoulders by Shelley Beeching.

'That was why you found me such a strange companion, Mr Faraday. And why I had to be so cagey with you.'

I nodded.

'I can understand that. But there are some other things I can't understand.'

'We'll get to those in a moment,' Ingolstadt said hastily.

The old lawyer exchanged a long look with Madsen.

'Most of this will come out, anyway,' he said. 'We have been unethical, it is true. But we had to bend the rules to get one of the biggest threats to law and order the State of California has ever known.'

'Sure,' Madsen said carelessly. 'But I guess we'll ride it out. A new broom has swept clean, for once.'

He grinned at the carnage around us.

'Did we get Comstock?'

He was talking to a big police Captain who'd just come in. The officer, who looked about eight feet tall in the dim light of the torches in here, grinned happily.

'He's being held the other side of the lake. Badly wounded, but he'll recover to stand trial. We got enough charges against him to hang him three times over.'

'Sternwood reacted like we thought he would,' the old lawyer went on. 'We heard through our grapevine he was out to get Madsen and Jenny Holm together. The thing

197

was so important he decided to handle it himself. We'd banked on this, of course. The whole operation was designed to get Sternwood and most of his trigger-men, including his heir-apparent, Comstock. Fortunately for us, the two decided to join forces against the new D.A.'

'All right,' I said. 'The secrecy was necessary. But why keep me in the dark?'

Madsen smiled thinly, the smoke from his cigarette coiling up slowly toward the dome.

'If we'd levelled with you, would you have taken the case?' he said. 'A lone P.I. going up against Sternwood and his mob?'

I stared at him for a long moment.

'Maybe not,' I said at last.

All the anger was seeping out of me. I could understand a great many things now. The girl making sure the bug was under the car; her sometimes strange and disconnected conversation; all the anomalies about her character; my unease about Ingolstadt and the whole operation.

'But we had to be extremely careful,' Madsen said. 'We didn't tell either of you the exact location of this place, for example. We'd chosen it carefully and got the whole area staked out with the police, State Troopers and helicopters as back-up. But one breath of what was involved to Sternwood and his boys would have been disastrous. And if they'd caught up with you, neither of you would have been able to tell Sternwood our complete plans.'

'We were expendable,' I said. 'If we'd been killed you'd have tried again.'

Madsen nodded, his lips drawn together in a thin line.

'You bet we would, Mr Faraday. This is a war we're engaged in.'

I stubbed out my cigarette on the top of the table. I took another drag of the laced coffee. I felt empty and drained. I couldn't even get into an argument with Ingolstadt. I looked at Lauren Jefferies' white face. She'd been prepared to stake her life on the operation. So had I, come to that, even though I hadn't known everything that was involved.

'You came through all right in the end,' I said to Madsen. 'You saved my life at any rate.'

He grinned.

'It was the least I could do.'

I glanced across at Ingolstadt.

'You haven't explained yet about the electronic bug under the car.'

'Ah, there we had to be extremely careful, Mr Faraday. The thing took some setting up, of course, but we have many contacts. As you may know it was impossible for a busy lawyer like myself to keep all my activities secret from a man like Sternwood. It was a matter of delicate balance; a mixture of probabilities. It took months to arrange and execute and I won't bother you with all the details. We had to make the opposition think they were putting it

199

across us. There were simulated leaks from Police H.Q. in New York in which we let it be known that Jenny Holm was coming west to testify. That was when we hired you, Mr Faraday, quite openly.'

'Knowing that I'd be a clay-pigeon,' I said.

'That's right,' Ingolstadt said happily. 'We gave you a dummy run, with some fake evidence. The strength and violence of Sternwood's reaction convinced us that he'd taken the bait.'

I opened my mouth to speak but Shelley Beeching stopped me.

'We've been all through that, Mr Faraday,' she said crisply. 'And you didn't get killed so all's well.'

'If you say so,' I said.

'I got Shelley to arrange for a hire-car,' Ingolstadt continued. 'We didn't conceal anything and we booked it several weeks in advance, so that anyone who went through the hire-car firm's books could put things together.'

'I don't understand,' I said.

Ingolstadt gave me a patient look.

'The car-hire outfit was a front, Mr Faraday. Or rather, it's a genuine firm but the man who owned it was Sternwood. We were sure he would bug it in some way.'

I stared at him incredulously.

'He could have blown us to fragments,' I said.

Ingolstadt shook his head.

'No way would we have allowed that, Mr Faraday. We had the finest electronic sensory equipment available to detect explosive. And we had one of our own men within the hire-firm who made sure nothing like that was planned. Besides, Sternwood wanted to get Madsen, not just Jenny Holm and a ten-a-penny private eye.'

'Don't under-rate me, Mr Ingolstadt,' I said. 'Two-a-penny, if you don't mind.'

The old man looked at me with a strange expression in his eyes.

'I'm not under-rating you, Mr Faraday. I don't think any other man in the world could have done what you did. You never put a foot wrong. That was because we let you believe everything we told you was the truth. We wanted you to be antagonistic to Jenny Holm and we wanted you to play everything by the book. You couldn't have acted nearly so well had you not believed what we told you, however much we wanted to level with you.'

'Maybe so,' I said.

I turned to look at the Jefferies girl.

'That was why you were checking on that bug in the garage. I thought you'd put it there but you had no more knowledge about it than I had.'

The girl shook her head, her eyes bright.

'I wanted to make sure we were leading Sternwood to the rendezvous, Mr Faraday.

There was no other reason. And I'm sorry I had to deceive you. My job was to make sure you thought we were afraid of Comstock, and that we were trying to shake him off.'

I grinned, all my animosity dropping away.

'You only half-deceived me, Mrs Smith. I already found out the scarf and the scar were fakes. Another day and I might have got hold of all the facts.'

'Then it was possibly a great mercy that the whole thing was wrapped up today,' said Ingolstadt softly.

His manner became brisk.

'We will all be lifted out of here by helicopter shortly. We will stay the night at a nearby hotel and fly back to L.A. in the morning. Miss Jefferies will be going to hospital for a check-up. I understand from the doctor there are not likely to be any complications and after a night's rest she should be fit to join us for the flight in the morning.'

We all got up and suddenly the dome was filled with police again and the tinny noise of portable radios. Ingolstadt took an envelope out his pocket and handed it me.

'What's this?' I said.

I opened it, stared at the mauve slip of paper it contained. The noughts seemed to go on for ever.

'I don't know what to say,' I said.

Ingolstadt snapped his mouth shut like a cuttle-fish.

'Try thank you,' he said.

Shelley Beeching and the Jefferies number smiled.

'You wrote that in the back room there,' I said.

Ingolstadt beamed.

'There is a small window and a table,' he said. 'It was an agreeable way of passing the time during the gun battle.'

I kept on staring at him.

'Without even knowing which way the thing was going to go?' I said. 'You would have been next.'

The old man shook his head.

'I think not, Mr Faraday,' he said softly. 'There were three of the best marksmen in the State up against Sternwood and the machine-gun artist.'

He smiled again.

'Besides, both Miss Beeching and myself were armed.'

He suddenly produced a Luger from his raincoat pocket, smiling at my expression.

'The legal profession in California can be dangerous too, Mr Faraday. Both Miss Beeching and I can shoot quite well. I wouldn't have given much for the chances of anyone trying to come through that door.'

I remembered the expression of the man with the bronze face as he'd gone down.

'You meant to get Sternwood, didn't you? It was an execution really.'

203

Ingolstadt's face had gone blank.

'A necessary one,' he said. 'Which you were also part of.'

He gestured round the dome.

'Besides this mausoleum was a not entirely inappropriate finale for him. And now he's gone to his long rest.'

I put the cheque in my pocket and looked round the dome. 'I could do with a long rest myself,' I said.

CHAPTER TWENTY-ONE

Grey light filled the interior of the small, two-engined air-craft as it circled L.A. International, waiting for permission to land. I looked across at Ingolstadt's smug face.

'You ripped me off all right,' I said.

He beamed even more victoriously.

'Come, Mr Faraday, don't talk nonsense. You are alive and well and considerably better off than you were a week ago, while the enemies of society are where they should be.'

Shelley Beeching gave a faint smile and Lauren Jefferies, who looked almost as good as new, despite her strapped-up arm, glanced tactfully out the window.

Ingolstadt had the brass to wink at me.

'You have a chance to rip me off now. You haven't made your expense account out yet.'

'You'll get it,' I promised him.

I thought of something else then.

'I'm glad it wasn't an out-of-town job,' I said. 'Else we might really have been in danger.'

I looked at the rain flecking the windows of the cabin and rolling down to make an impenetrable mist on the glass.

'I haven't forgiven you for all that lost sleep yet,' I told Ingolstadt.

He grinned.

'We had to make it look real to Sternwood, Mr Faraday. All that twisting and turning was vitally necessary.'

'You were tuned in to the bug too,' I said.

'Naturally,' he said.

I looked at Madsen.

'That was your house being built up on the bluff, wasn't it?'

He nodded, the ice-blue eyes looking thoughtful.

'You could have gotten out all right the other end, Mr Faraday. We wouldn't have sent you into anything as lethal as that.'

'Something still puzzles me,' I said.

'Be my guest,' Ingolstadt said.

'We've never discussed it,' I said. 'But if Sternwood had tried to disfigure Jenny Holm, why would she give evidence for him? I tried the question out on Miss Jefferies here but the answer wasn't very satisfactory.'

'Real life is never very satisfactory, Mr

Faraday,' Ingolstadt said smoothly. 'We tried the question out on the real Jenny Holm. She didn't know the true facts, of course. But she was quite willing to make the journey the Lieutenant took with you if it would have saved Sternwood from the gallows.'

'And you left the small door in the dome open to make Sternwood think Madsen was hiding up there? And that selection of boats at the lake?'

'Of course, Mr Faraday. I think we thought of pretty well everything.'

'Yeah, it was a nicely planned execution,' I said.

Ingolstadt put on his stiff manner again. Madsen was sitting facing in front of him. He kept a discreet silence.

Ingolstadt shrugged. Shelley Beeching bit her lip as she looked at me. She was getting pretty good at that.

'It was them or us,' Ingolstadt said bleakly.

The plane was banking now, turning in to land. The buildings of L.A. International slid by under the port wing, grey and anonymous in the sheeting rain. We landed in a remote area and taxied down to where police and other officials were waiting in a discreet knot to greet the new D.A.

Lauren Jefferies was helped out first. She gave me her uninjured hand to shake.

'It was quite an experience, Mr Faraday.'

'You can say that again,' I said.

The door of the plane was opened and the steps racked down. Ingolstadt beamed around him like he'd just had a good day at the races.

'Remember, Mr Faraday,' he said. 'We're having a celebratory dinner this evening. Just you and me and Shelley and your own young lady.'

'If you insist,' I said.

'I do insist, my boy.'

He was back to his Lionel Barrymore manner again. I absorbed what he said about the restaurant and the time. All the while I was searching the faces below. Suddenly I saw her standing alone at the edge of the crowd. Stella looked great. She wore a dark red raincoat with an absurd little white hat that looked like a mushroom on top of the blonde bell of her hair. She smiled gravely and held up her hand to her eyes as I went down the gangway.

I caught Shelley Beeching's expression. She looked at me, the corners of her mouth turned down in a little gesture of regret.

'Don't let her get away, Mr Faraday,' she said softly.

'I won't,' I told her.

Stella put up her forehead to be kissed in the falling rain.

'You came out on top again,' she said.

'Sort of,' I said. 'I was conned all the way through.'

'So's the whole world,' she said. 'But you get paid for it.'

I grinned. She had a point. She took me by the arm and steered me through the crowd.

'Your heap or mine?'

'Mine first,' I said. 'It's been here two days. I want to make sure it's still here.'

We were up near the gate where I'd left the Buick by now. The rain slashed down but I hardly felt it. I found the car-park, worked my way down, Stella following. I got up near and stopped. There was a big cop standing there with a red-haired policewoman who looked as tall and as durable as a Russian commissar. He pointed accusingly at the Buick's side-window.

'That's definitely a bullet-hole,' he said aggressively. 'And there's a big dent on the bonnet there. Get back to the car and report the licence details while I check this name and address.'

I turned on my heel and came back. Stella was smiling.

'We'll take my heap. Let Ingolstadt and Madsen sort it out.'

I nodded.

'It will be something else on Ingolstadt's expense account.'

Stella didn't say anything but on the way back into town she started laughing.

We hope you have enjoyed this Large Print book. Other Chivers Press or Thorndike Press Large Print books are available at your library or directly from the publishers. For more information about current and forthcoming titles, please call or write, without obligation, to:

Chivers Press Limited
Windsor Bridge Road
Bath BA2 3AX
England
Tel. (0225) 335336

OR

Thorndike Press
P.O. Box 159
Thorndike, ME 04986
USA
Tel. (800) 223-6121
(207) 948-2962
(in Maine and Canada, call collect)

All our Large Print titles are designed for easy reading, and all our books are made to last.